THE UNDERGROUND ADVENTURE OF ARLY DUNBAR,

CAVE EXPLORER

BY **CANDICE RANSOM**
ADAPTED BY **EMMA CARLSON BERNE**
ILLUSTRATED BY **TED HAMMOND** AND **RICHARD PIMENTEL CARBAJAL**

Graphic Universe™ • Minneapolis • New York

INTRODUCTION

ON JANUARY 30, 1925, FLOYD COLLINS CRAWLED INTO A CAVERN CALLED SAND CAVE. AT AGE 37, FLOYD WAS USED TO EXPLORING CAVES. CAVE CITY, HIS HOME IN CENTRAL KENTUCKY, HAD MANY UNDERGROUND CAVERNS.

THAT COLD FRIDAY NIGHT, FLOYD SLITHERED INTO SAND CAVE'S NARROW TUNNEL. HE CARRIED ONLY A KEROSENE LANTERN AND A LENGTH OF ROPE. HE WRIGGLED AND SQUEEZED UNTIL HE WAS 55 FEET FROM THE ENTRANCE. SUDDENLY, HIS LANTERN TIPPED AND WENT OUT. FLOYD KICKED AGAINST A LIMESTONE ROCK. PART OF THE ROCK FELL ON HIS LEFT FOOT. THEN A SHOWER OF ROCKS AND DIRT FELL ON HIS LEGS, COVERING THEM.

FLOYD WAS TRAPPED.

THE NEXT DAY, FLOYD'S NEIGHBORS AND RELATIVES FOUND HIM. BUT NO ONE COULD FREE HIM. THE TUNNEL WAS TOO SMALL FOR ANYONE TO DIG HIM OUT. BUT MANY PEOPLE—INCLUDING MEMBERS OF THE NATIONAL GUARD—TRIED TO HELP. SOON, WORD OF FLOYD'S SITUATION GOT THE PUBLIC'S ATTENTION. NEWSPEOPLE FLOCKED TO THE SITE.

THIS IS THE STORY OF WHAT HAPPENED AT SAND CAVE. TEN-YEAR-OLD ARLY DUNBAR IS NOT A REAL PERSON. BUT THE DANGER THAT FLOYD COLLINS FACED IS TRUE.

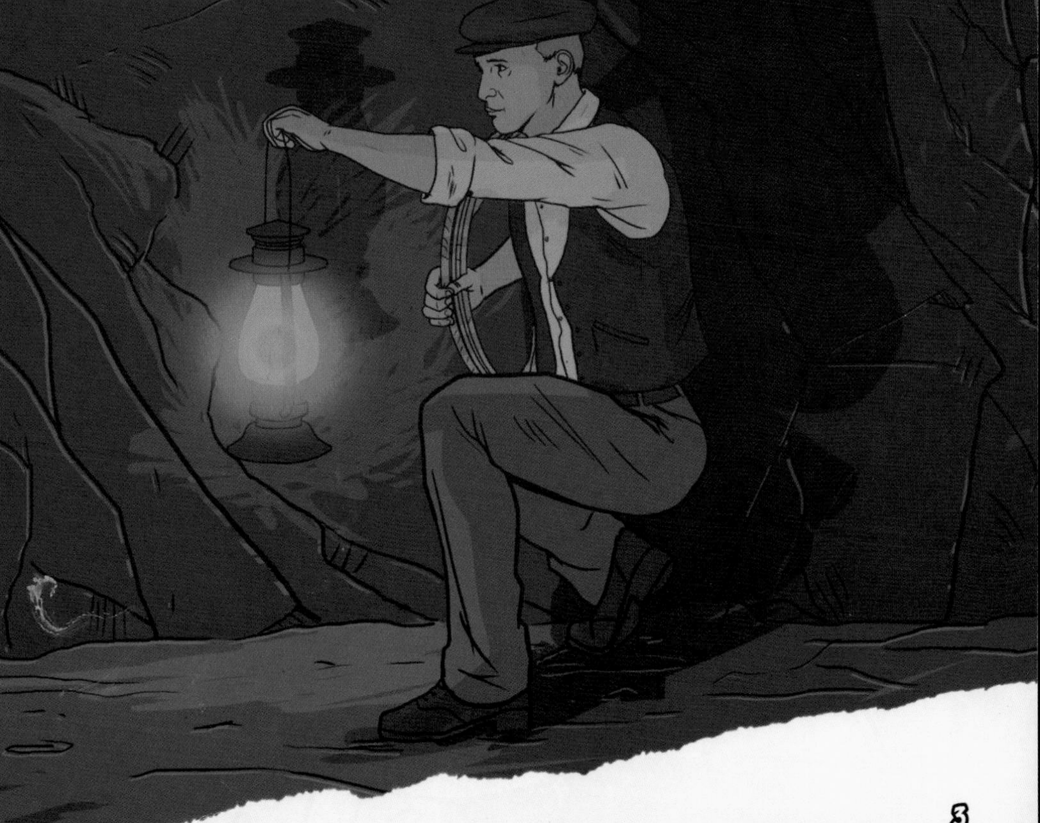

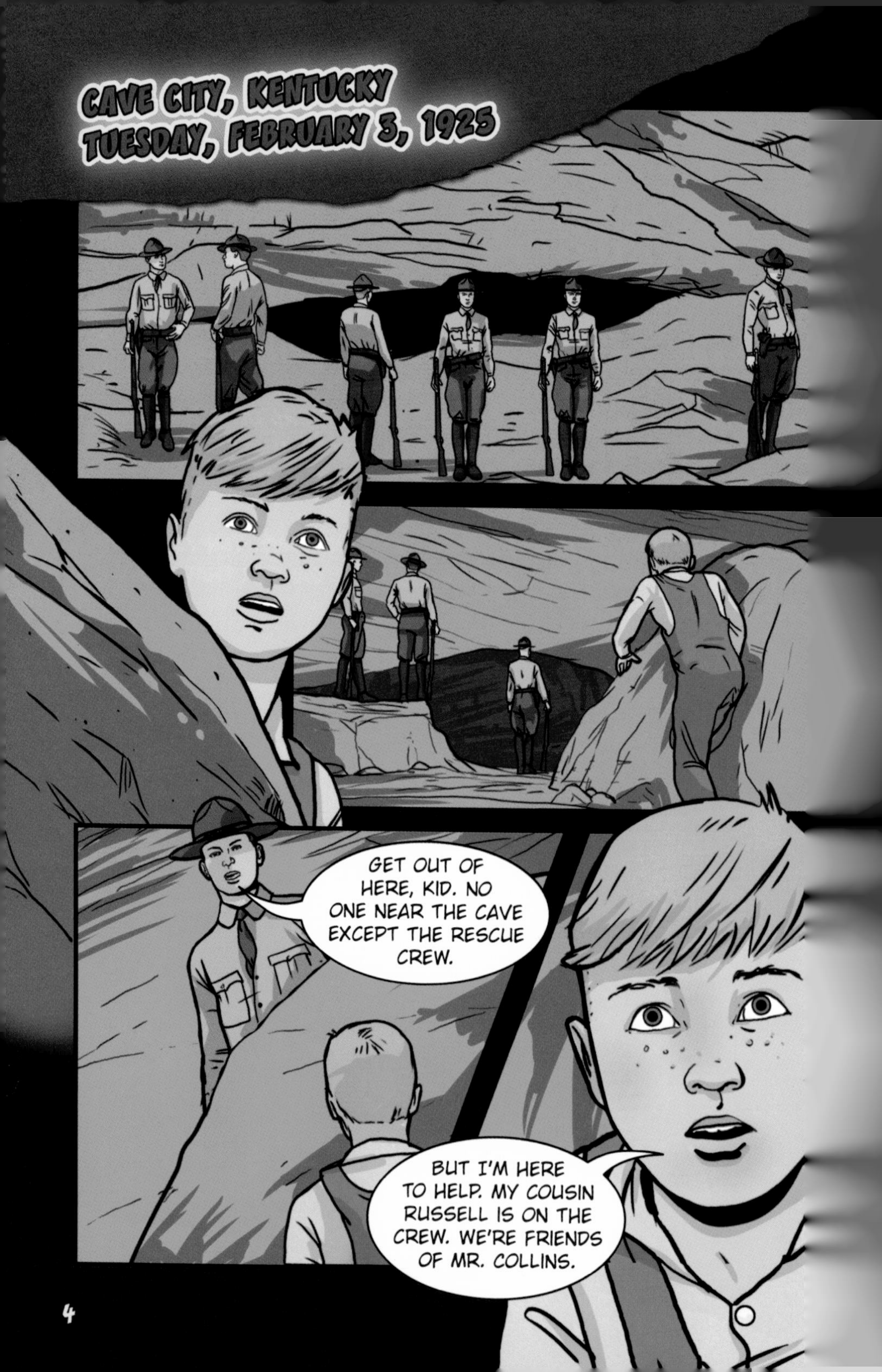
CAVE CITY, KENTUCKY
TUESDAY, FEBRUARY 3, 1925
GET OUT OF HERE, KID. NO ONE NEAR THE CAVE EXCEPT THE RESCUE CREW.
BUT I'M HERE TO HELP. MY COUSIN RUSSELL IS ON THE CREW. WE'RE FRIENDS OF MR. COLLINS.

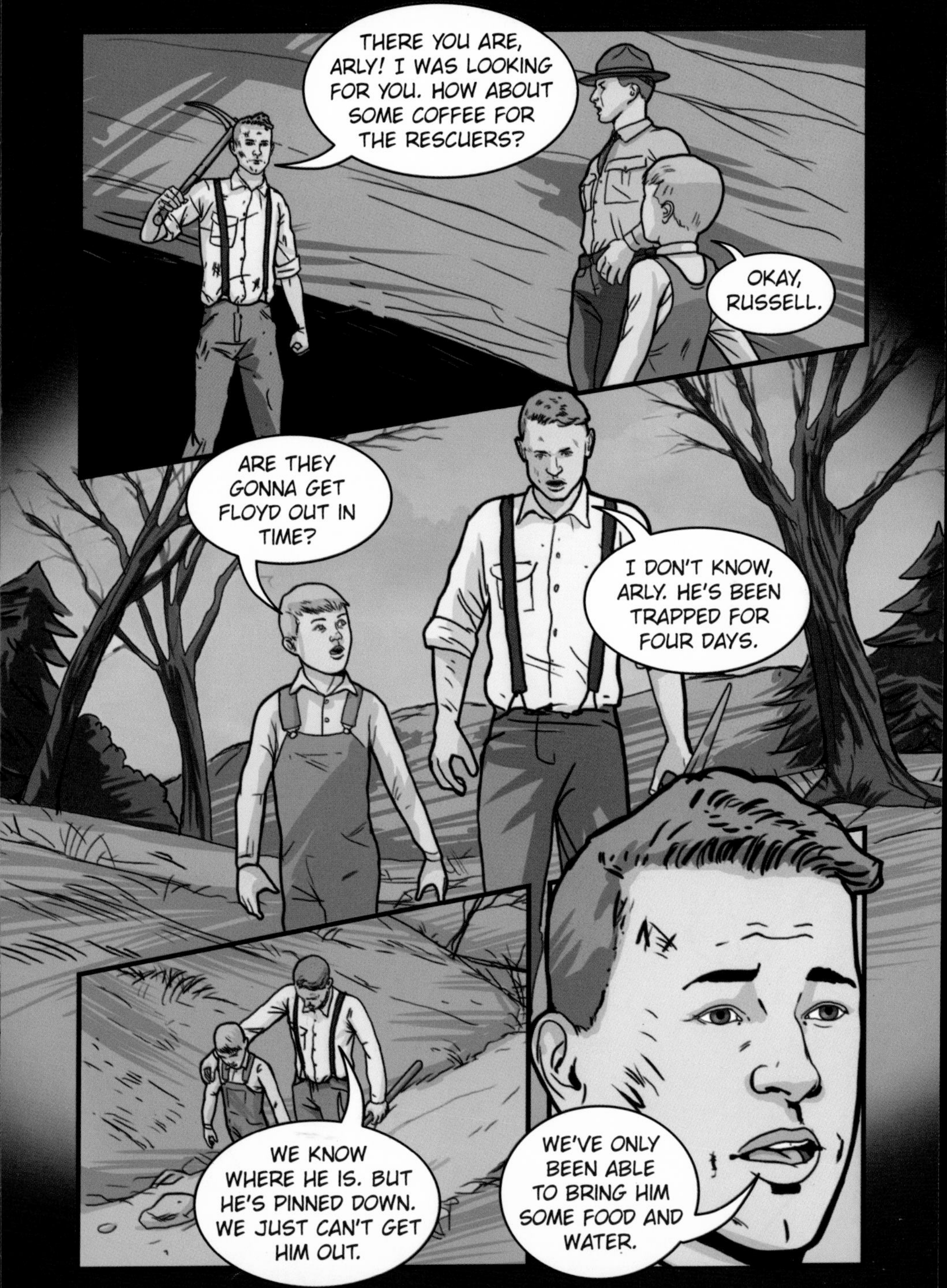
THERE YOU ARE, ARLY! I WAS LOOKING FOR YOU. HOW ABOUT SOME COFFEE FOR THE RESCUERS?
OKAY, RUSSELL.
ARE THEY GONNA GET FLOYD OUT IN TIME?
I DON'T KNOW, ARLY. HE'S BEEN TRAPPED FOR FOUR DAYS.
WE KNOW WHERE HE IS. BUT HE'S PINNED DOWN. WE JUST CAN'T GET HIM OUT.
WE'VE ONLY BEEN ABLE TO BRING HIM SOME FOOD AND WATER.

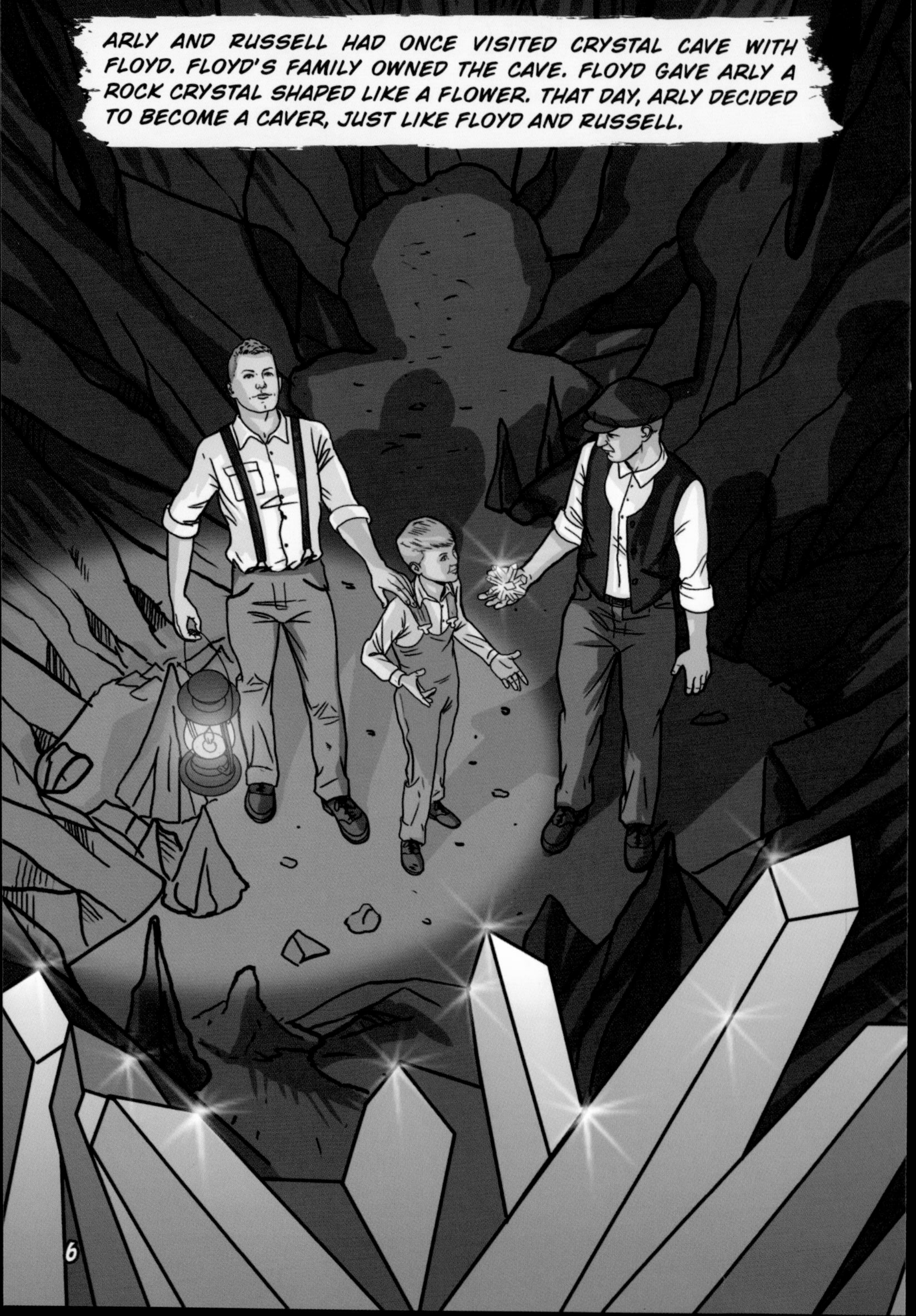
ARLY AND RUSSELL HAD ONCE VISITED CRYSTAL CAVE WITH FLOYD. FLOYD'S FAMILY OWNED THE CAVE. FLOYD GAVE ARLY A ROCK CRYSTAL SHAPED LIKE A FLOWER. THAT DAY, ARLY DECIDED TO BECOME A CAVER, JUST LIKE FLOYD AND RUSSELL.

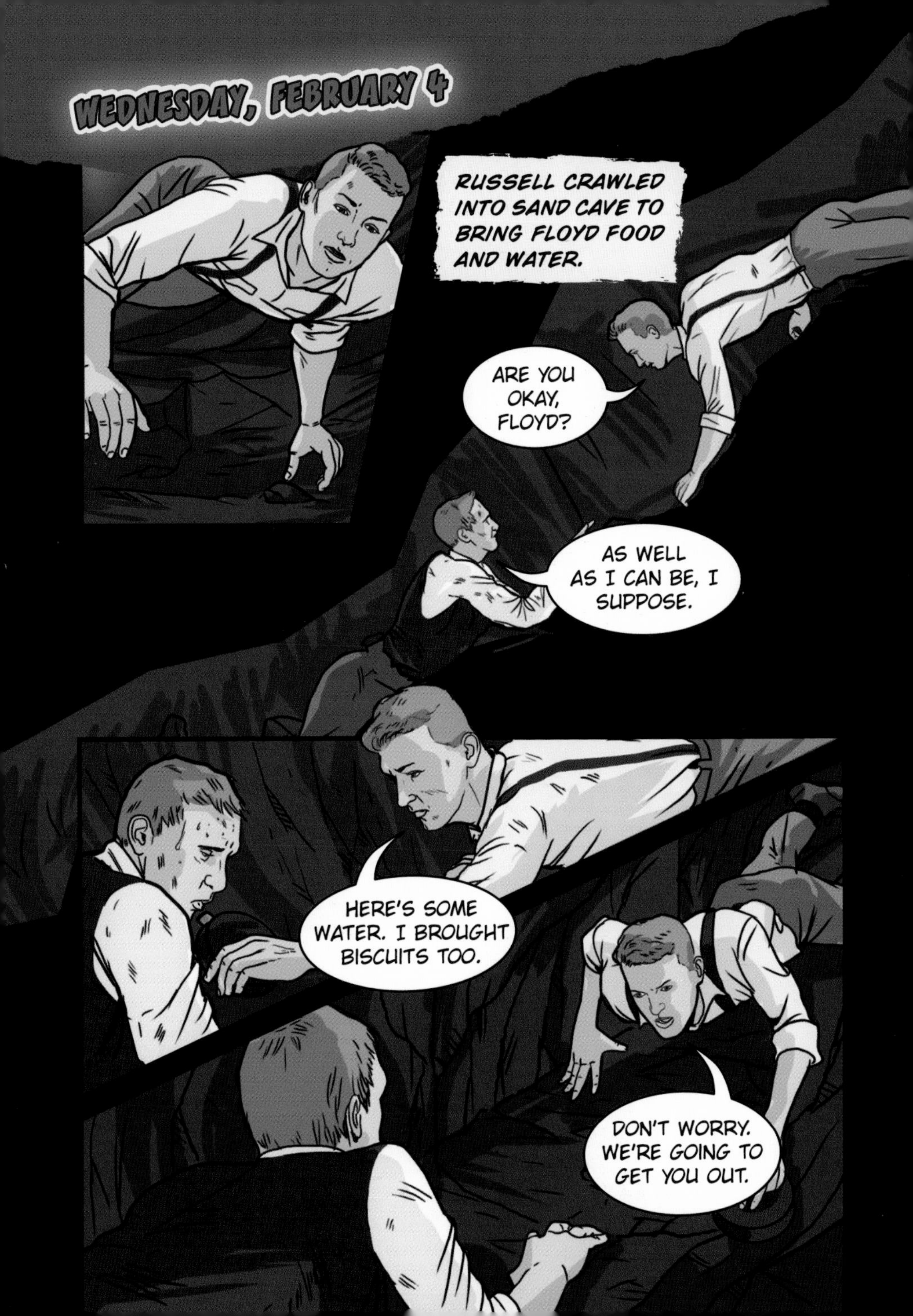
WEDNESDAY, FEBRUARY 4
RUSSELL CRAWLED INTO SAND CAVE TO BRING FLOYD FOOD AND WATER.
ARE YOU OKAY, FLOYD?
AS WELL AS I CAN BE, I SUPPOSE.
HERE'S SOME WATER. I BROUGHT BISCUITS TOO.
DON'T WORRY. WE'RE GOING TO GET YOU OUT.

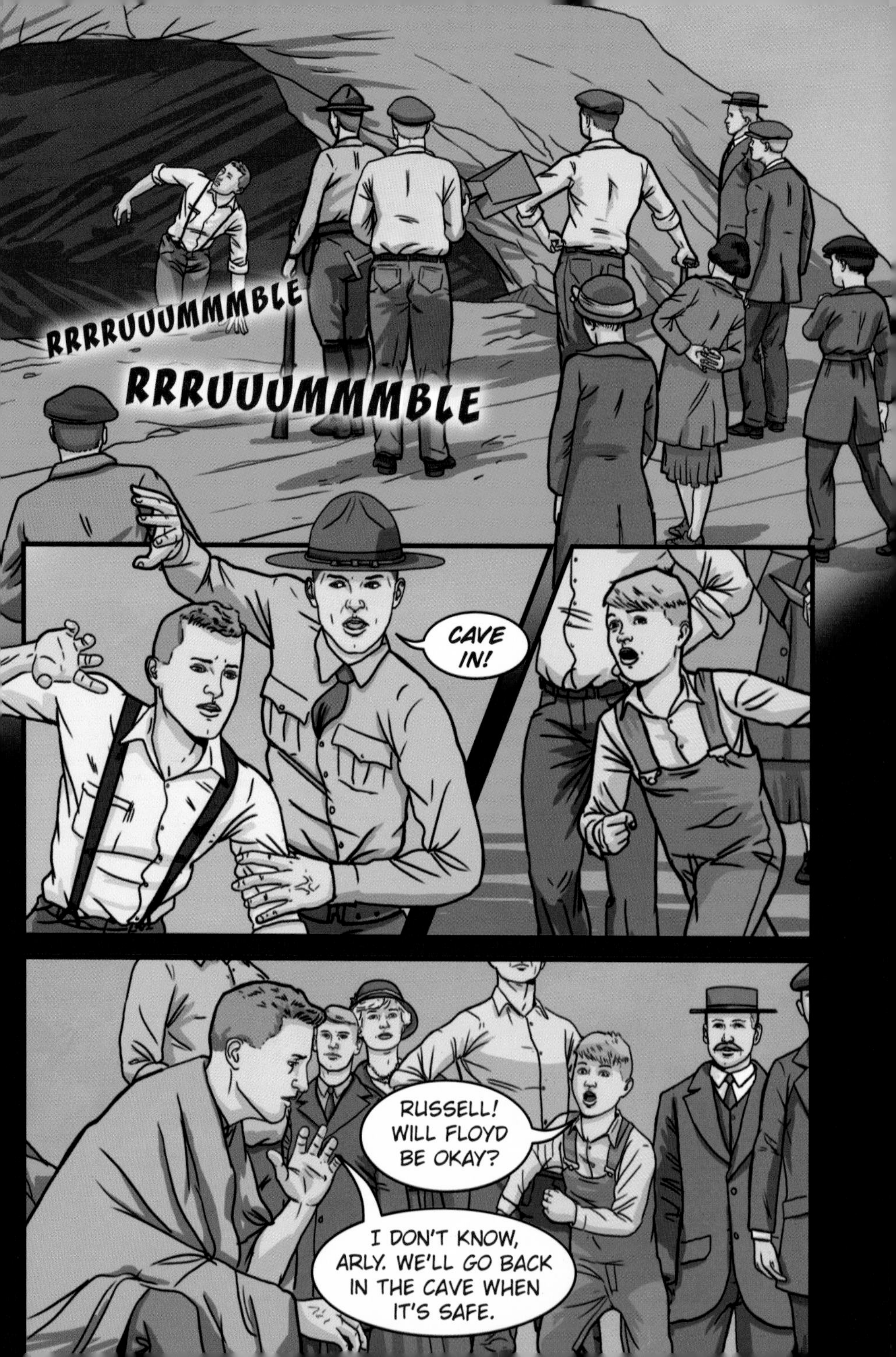
RRRRUUUMMMBLE
RRRUUUMMMBLE
CAVE IN!
RUSSELL! WILL FLOYD BE OKAY?
I DON'T KNOW, ARLY. WE'LL GO BACK IN THE CAVE WHEN IT'S SAFE.

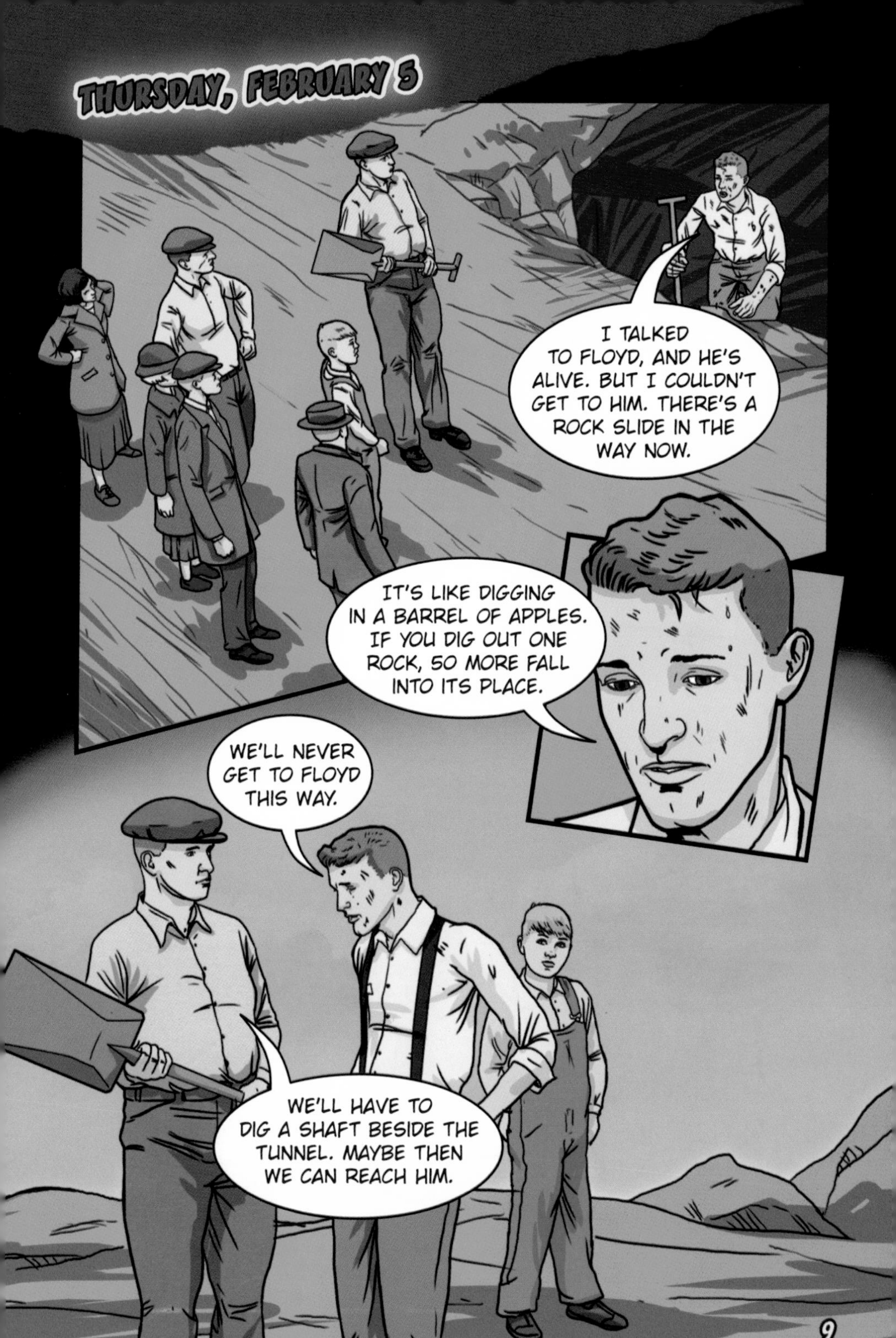
THURSDAY, FEBRUARY 5
I TALKED TO FLOYD, AND HE'S ALIVE. BUT I COULDN'T GET TO HIM. THERE'S A ROCK SLIDE IN THE WAY NOW.
IT'S LIKE DIGGING IN A BARREL OF APPLES. IF YOU DIG OUT ONE ROCK, 50 MORE FALL INTO ITS PLACE.
WE'LL NEVER GET TO FLOYD THIS WAY.
WE'LL HAVE TO DIG A SHAFT BESIDE THE TUNNEL. MAYBE THEN WE CAN REACH HIM.

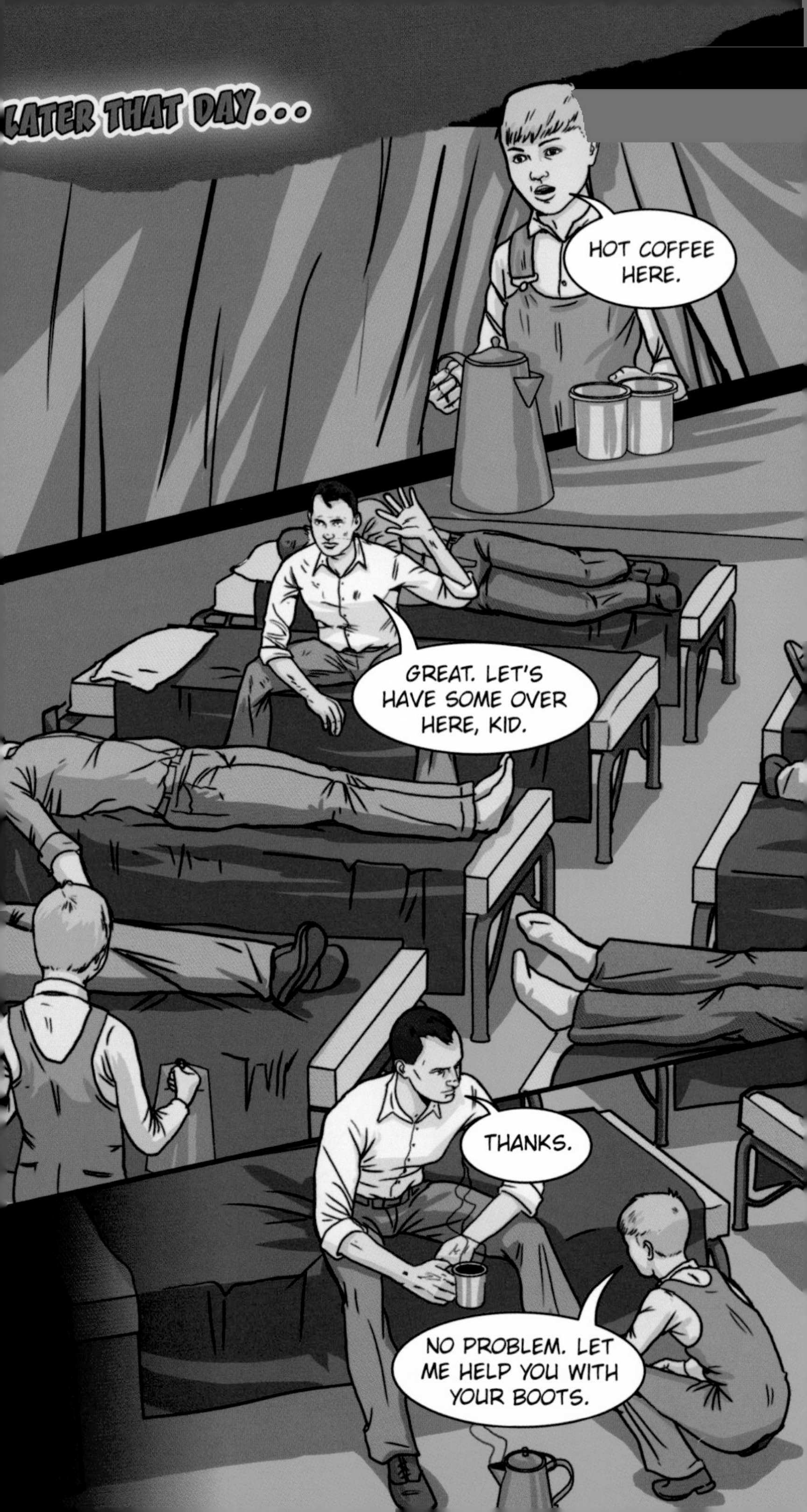
LATER THAT DAY...
HOT COFFEE HERE.
GREAT. LET'S HAVE SOME OVER HERE, KID.
THANKS.
NO PROBLEM. LET ME HELP YOU WITH YOUR BOOTS.

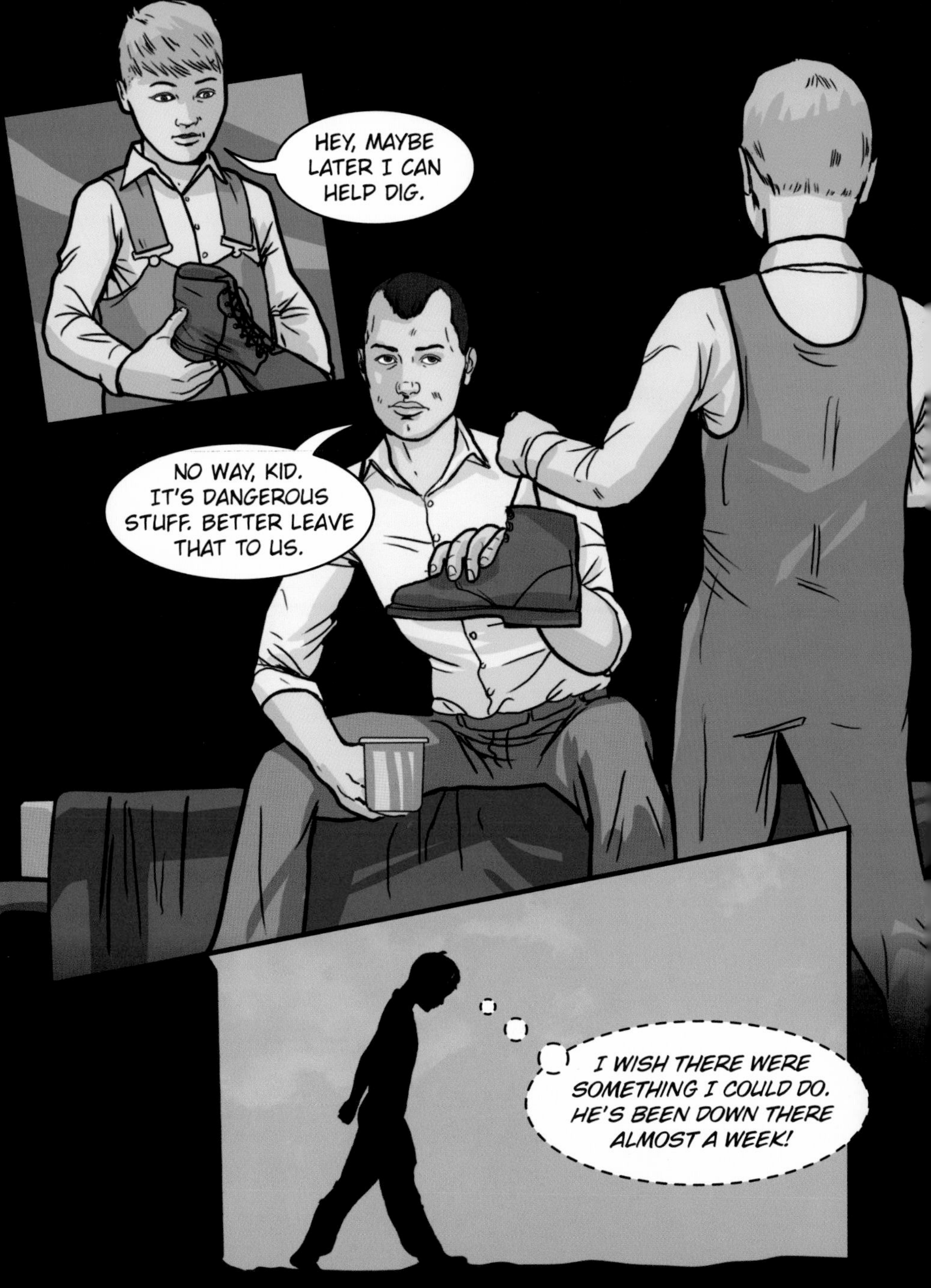
HEY, MAYBE LATER I CAN HELP DIG.
NO WAY, KID. IT'S DANGEROUS STUFF. BETTER LEAVE THAT TO US.
I WISH THERE WERE SOMETHING I COULD DO. HE'S BEEN DOWN THERE ALMOST A WEEK!

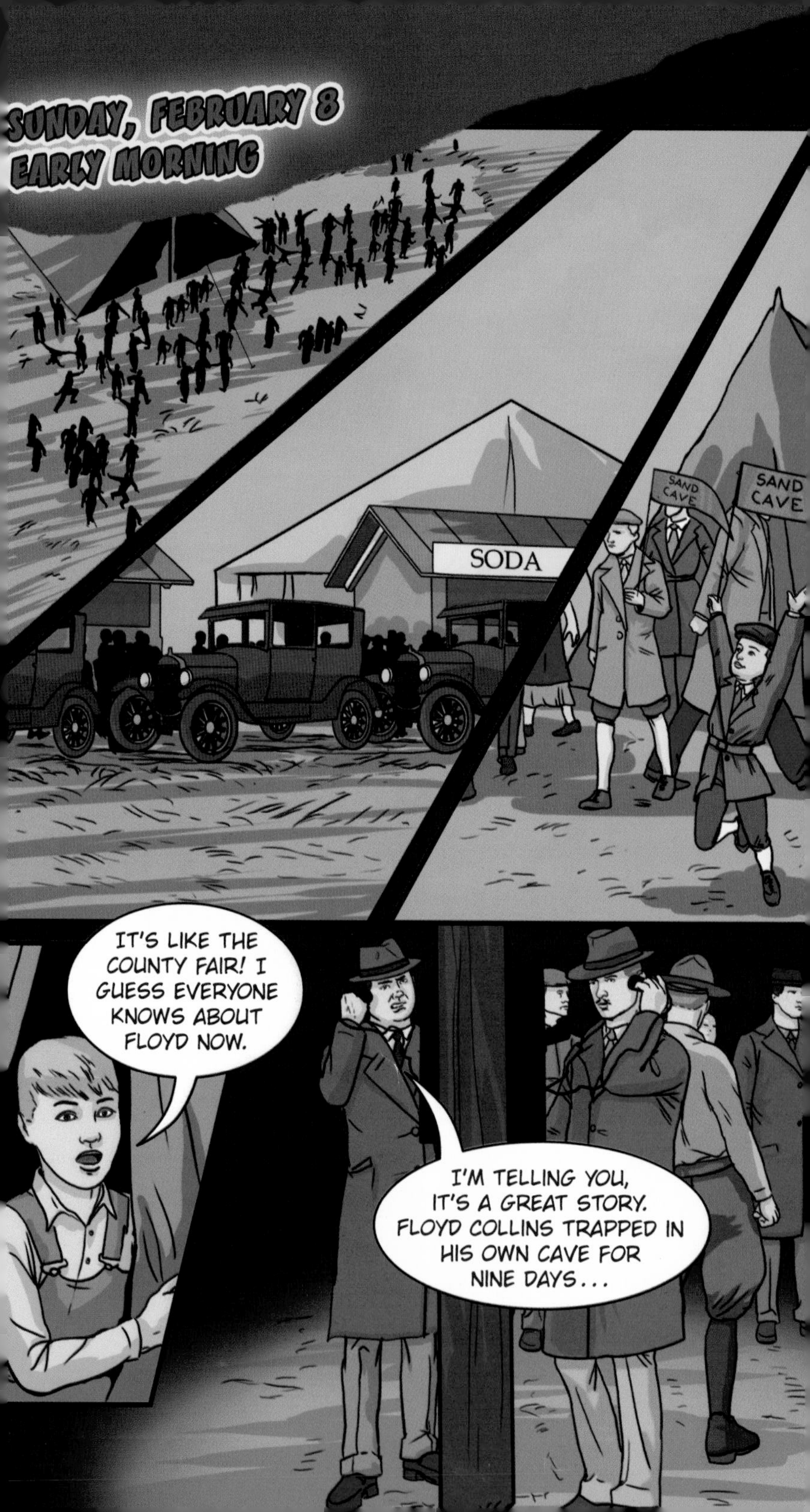
SUNDAY, FEBRUARY 8
EARLY MORNING
SODA
SAND CAVE
SAND CAVE
IT'S LIKE THE COUNTY FAIR! I GUESS EVERYONE KNOWS ABOUT FLOYD NOW.
I'M TELLING YOU, IT'S A GREAT STORY. FLOYD COLLINS TRAPPED IN HIS OWN CAVE FOR NINE DAYS . . .

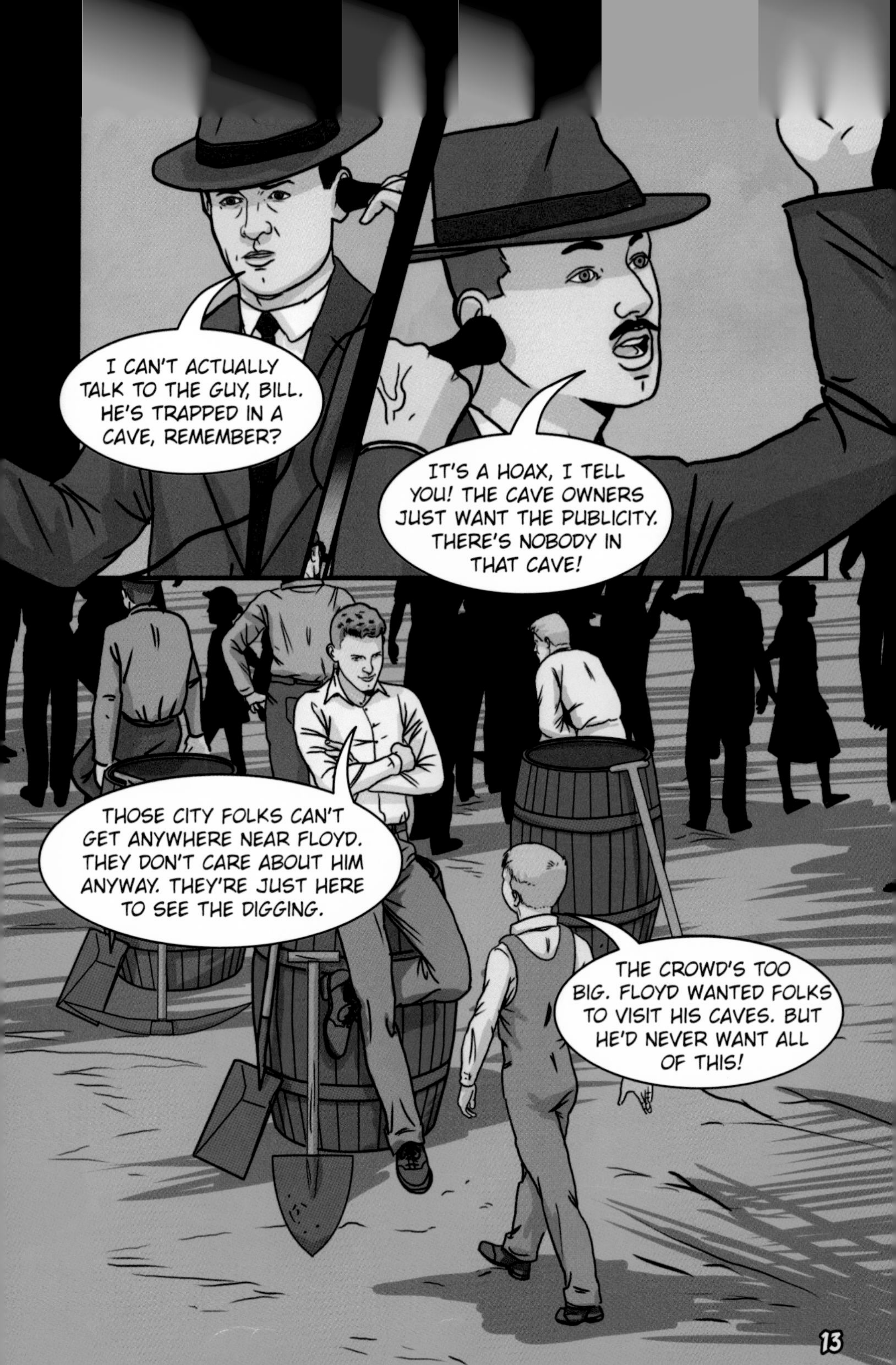
I CAN'T ACTUALLY TALK TO THE GUY, BILL. HE'S TRAPPED IN A CAVE, REMEMBER?
IT'S A HOAX, I TELL YOU! THE CAVE OWNERS JUST WANT THE PUBLICITY. THERE'S NOBODY IN THAT CAVE!
THOSE CITY FOLKS CAN'T GET ANYWHERE NEAR FLOYD. THEY DON'T CARE ABOUT HIM ANYWAY. THEY'RE JUST HERE TO SEE THE DIGGING.
THE CROWD'S TOO BIG. FLOYD WANTED FOLKS TO VISIT HIS CAVES. BUT HE'D NEVER WANT ALL OF THIS!

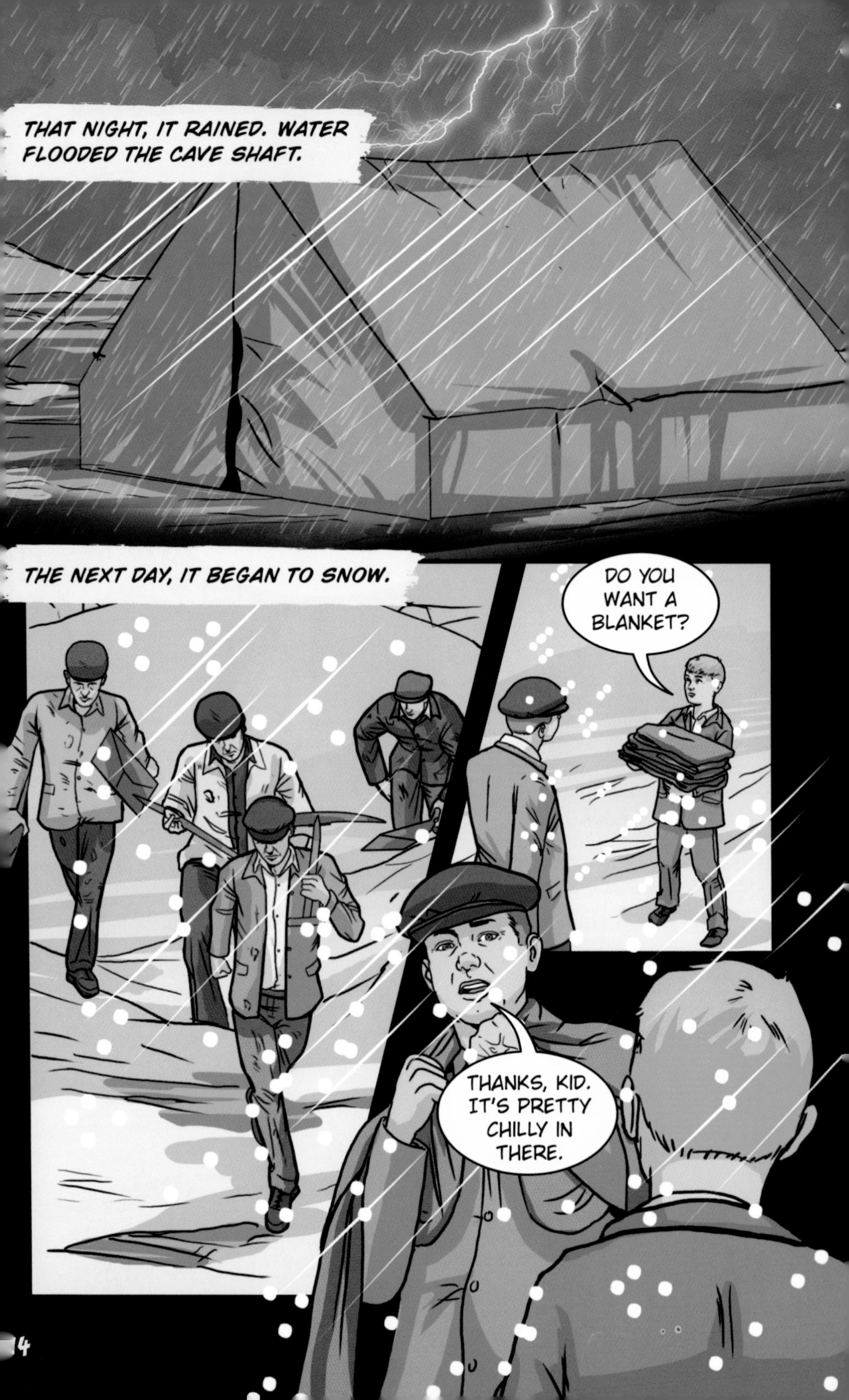
THAT NIGHT, IT RAINED. WATER FLOODED THE CAVE SHAFT.
THE NEXT DAY, IT BEGAN TO SNOW.
DO YOU WANT A BLANKET?
THANKS, KID. IT'S PRETTY CHILLY IN THERE.

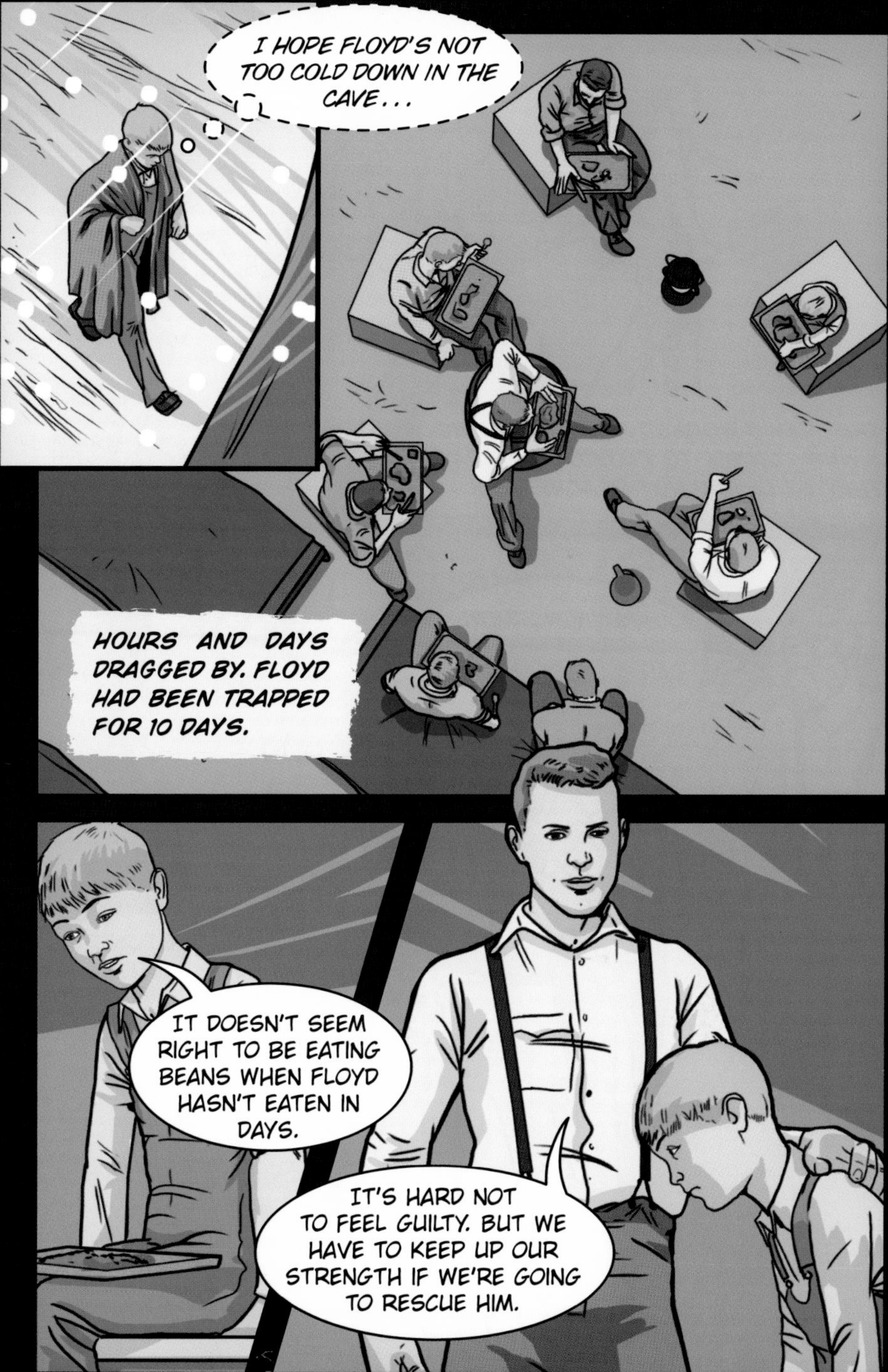
I HOPE FLOYD'S NOT TOO COLD DOWN IN THE CAVE . . .
HOURS AND DAYS DRAGGED BY. FLOYD HAD BEEN TRAPPED FOR 10 DAYS.
IT DOESN'T SEEM RIGHT TO BE EATING BEANS WHEN FLOYD HASN'T EATEN IN DAYS.
IT'S HARD NOT TO FEEL GUILTY. BUT WE HAVE TO KEEP UP OUR STRENGTH IF WE'RE GOING TO RESCUE HIM.

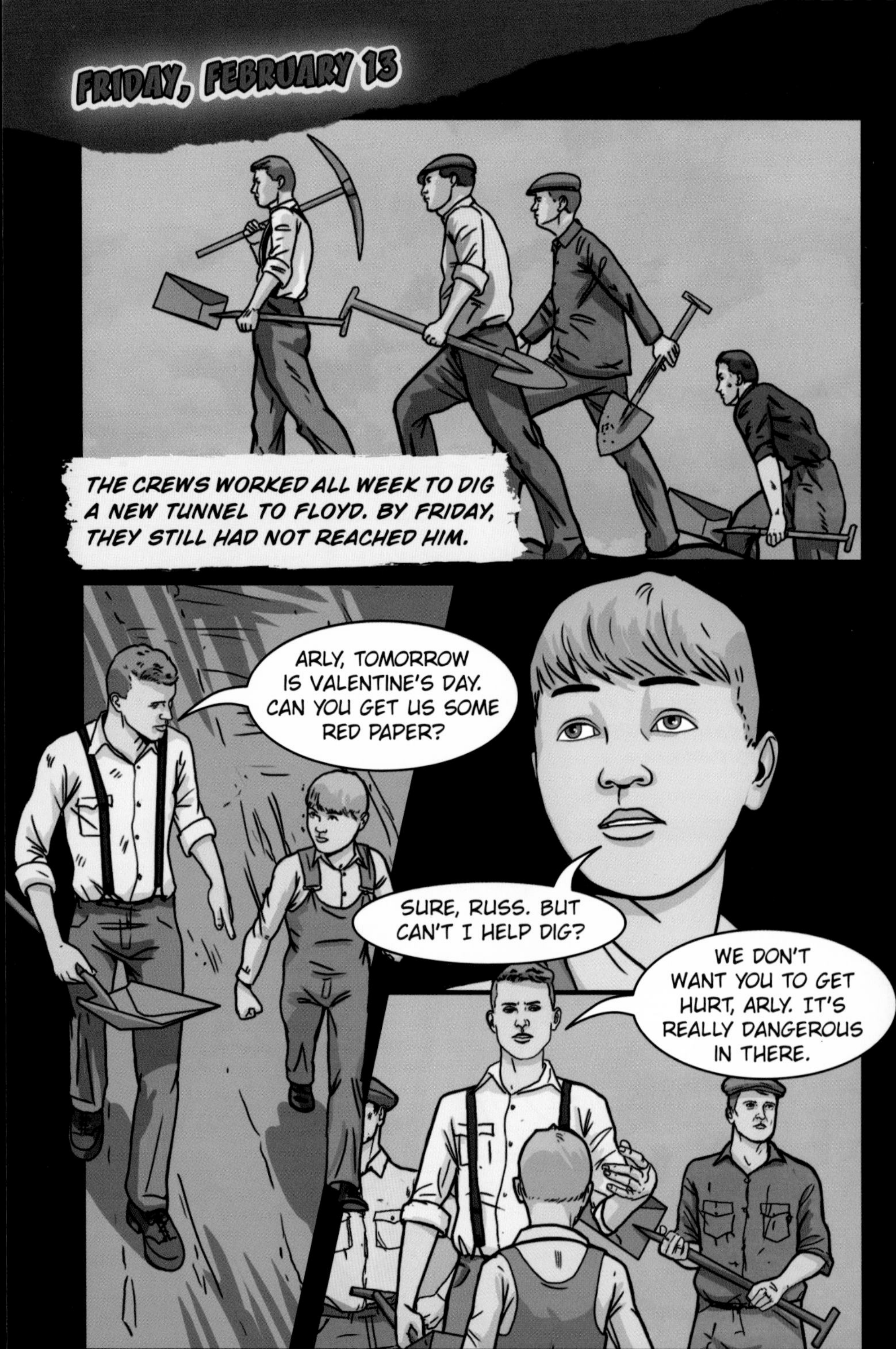
FRIDAY, FEBRUARY 13
THE CREWS WORKED ALL WEEK TO DIG A NEW TUNNEL TO FLOYD. BY FRIDAY, THEY STILL HAD NOT REACHED HIM.
ARLY, TOMORROW IS VALENTINE'S DAY. CAN YOU GET US SOME RED PAPER?
SURE, RUSS. BUT CAN'T I HELP DIG?
WE DON'T WANT YOU TO GET HURT, ARLY. IT'S REALLY DANGEROUS IN THERE.

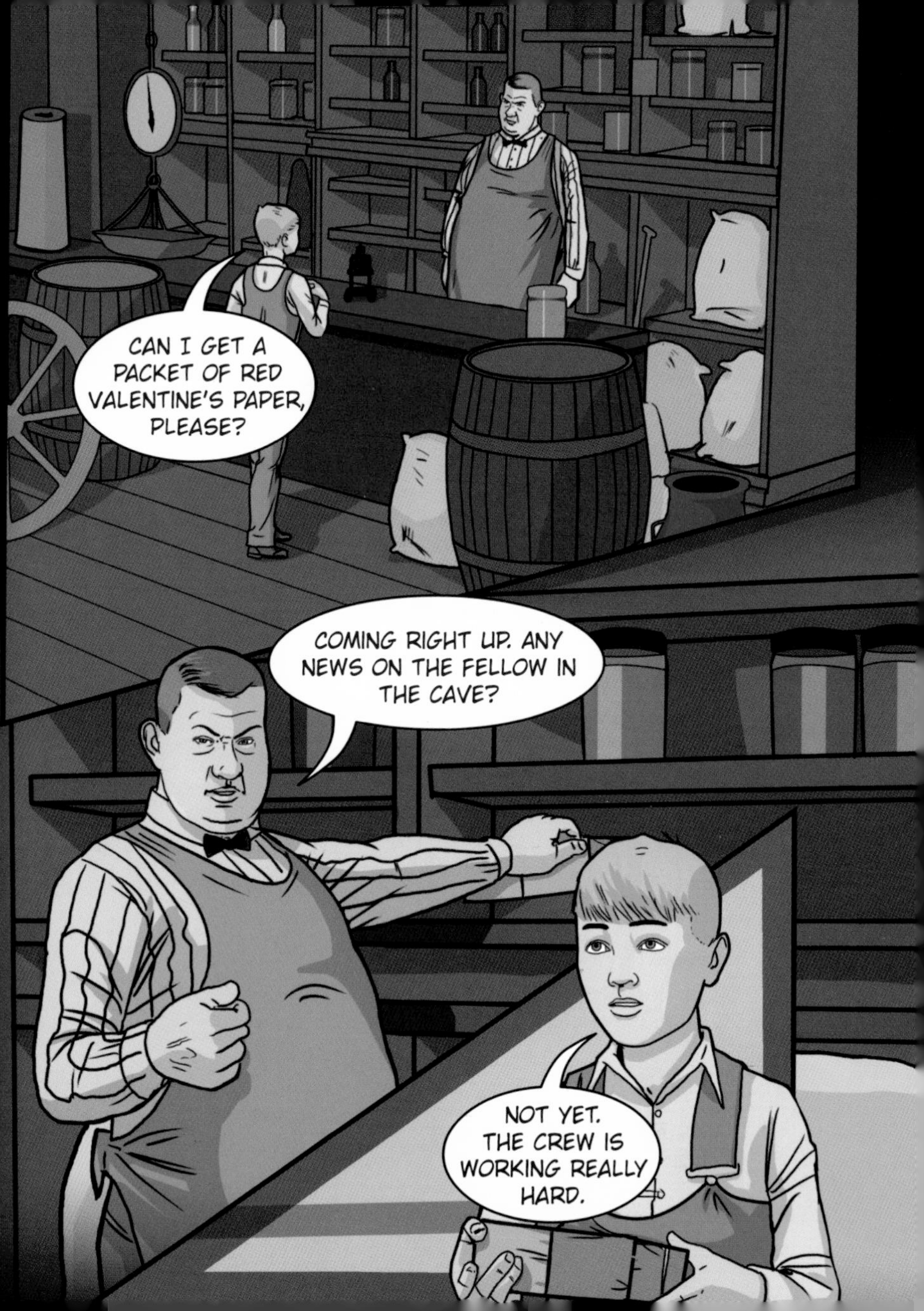
CAN I GET A PACKET OF RED VALENTINE'S PAPER, PLEASE?
COMING RIGHT UP. ANY NEWS ON THE FELLOW IN THE CAVE?
NOT YET. THE CREW IS WORKING REALLY HARD.

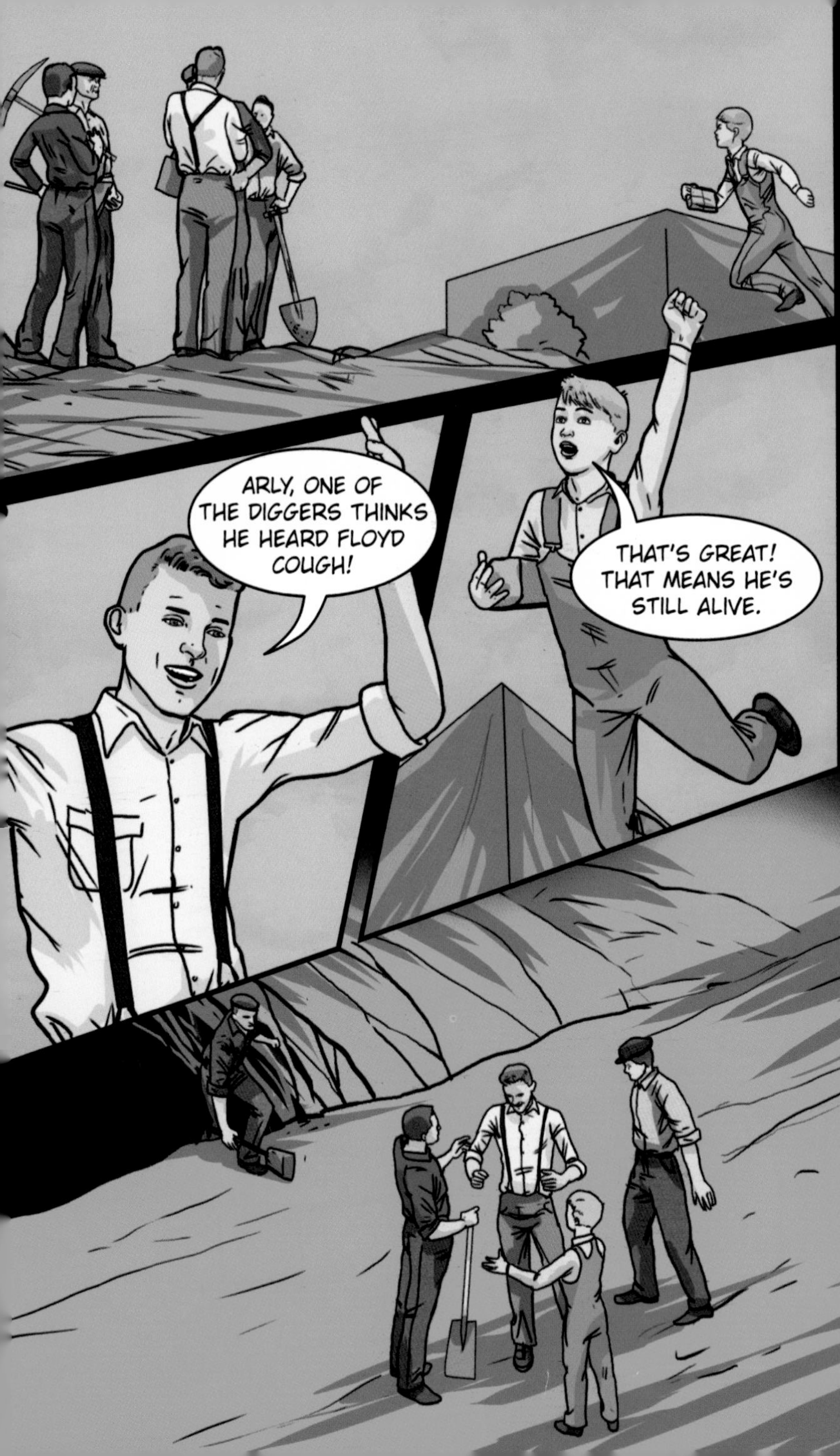
ARLY, ONE OF THE DIGGERS THINKS HE HEARD FLOYD COUGH!
THAT'S GREAT! THAT MEANS HE'S STILL ALIVE.

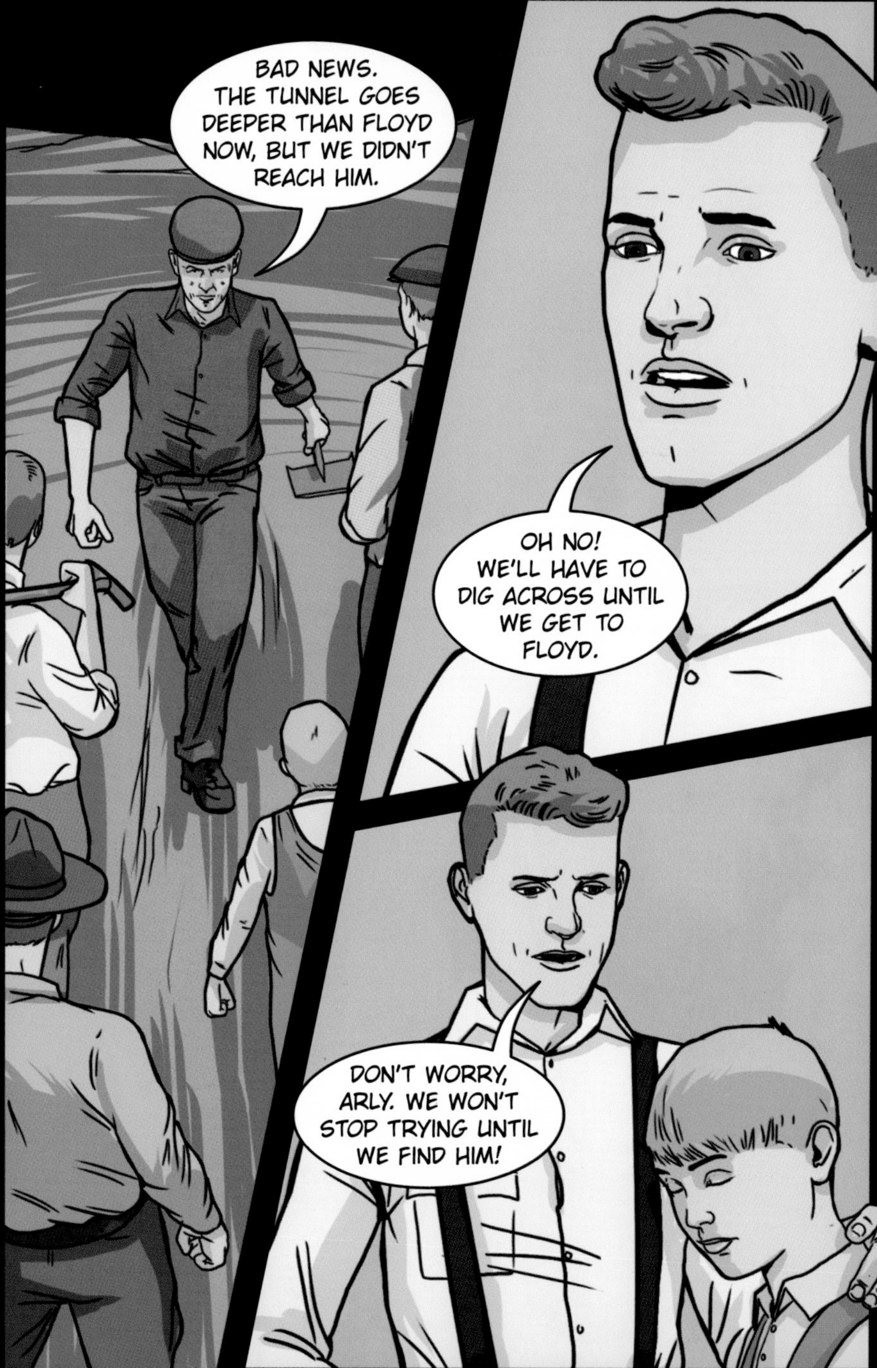
BAD NEWS. THE TUNNEL GOES DEEPER THAN FLOYD NOW, BUT WE DIDN'T REACH HIM.
OH NO! WE'LL HAVE TO DIG ACROSS UNTIL WE GET TO FLOYD.
DON'T WORRY, ARLY. WE WON'T STOP TRYING UNTIL WE FIND HIM!

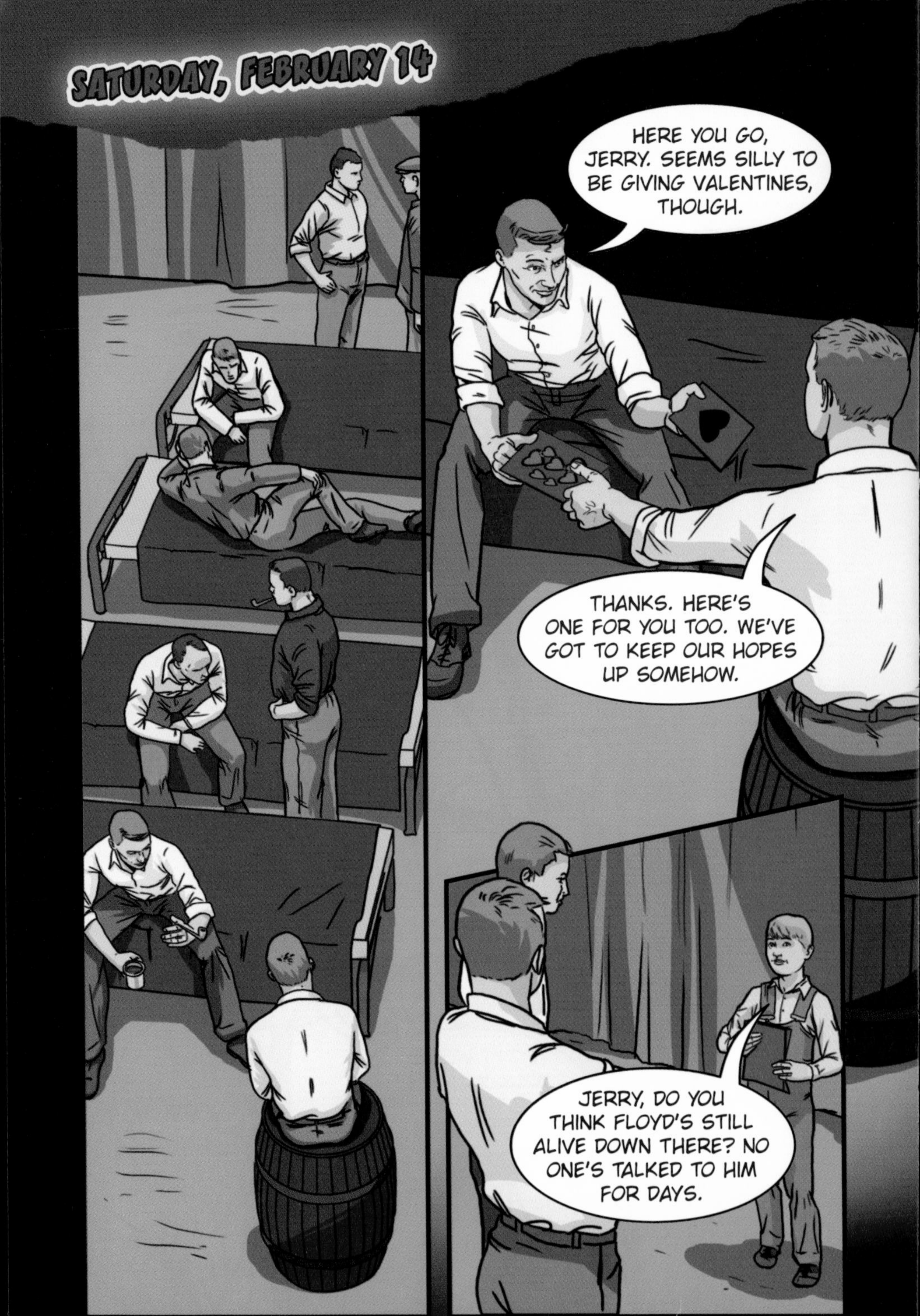
SATURDAY, FEBRUARY 14
HERE YOU GO, JERRY. SEEMS SILLY TO BE GIVING VALENTINES, THOUGH.
THANKS. HERE'S ONE FOR YOU TOO. WE'VE GOT TO KEEP OUR HOPES UP SOMEHOW.
JERRY, DO YOU THINK FLOYD'S STILL ALIVE DOWN THERE? NO ONE'S TALKED TO HIM FOR DAYS.

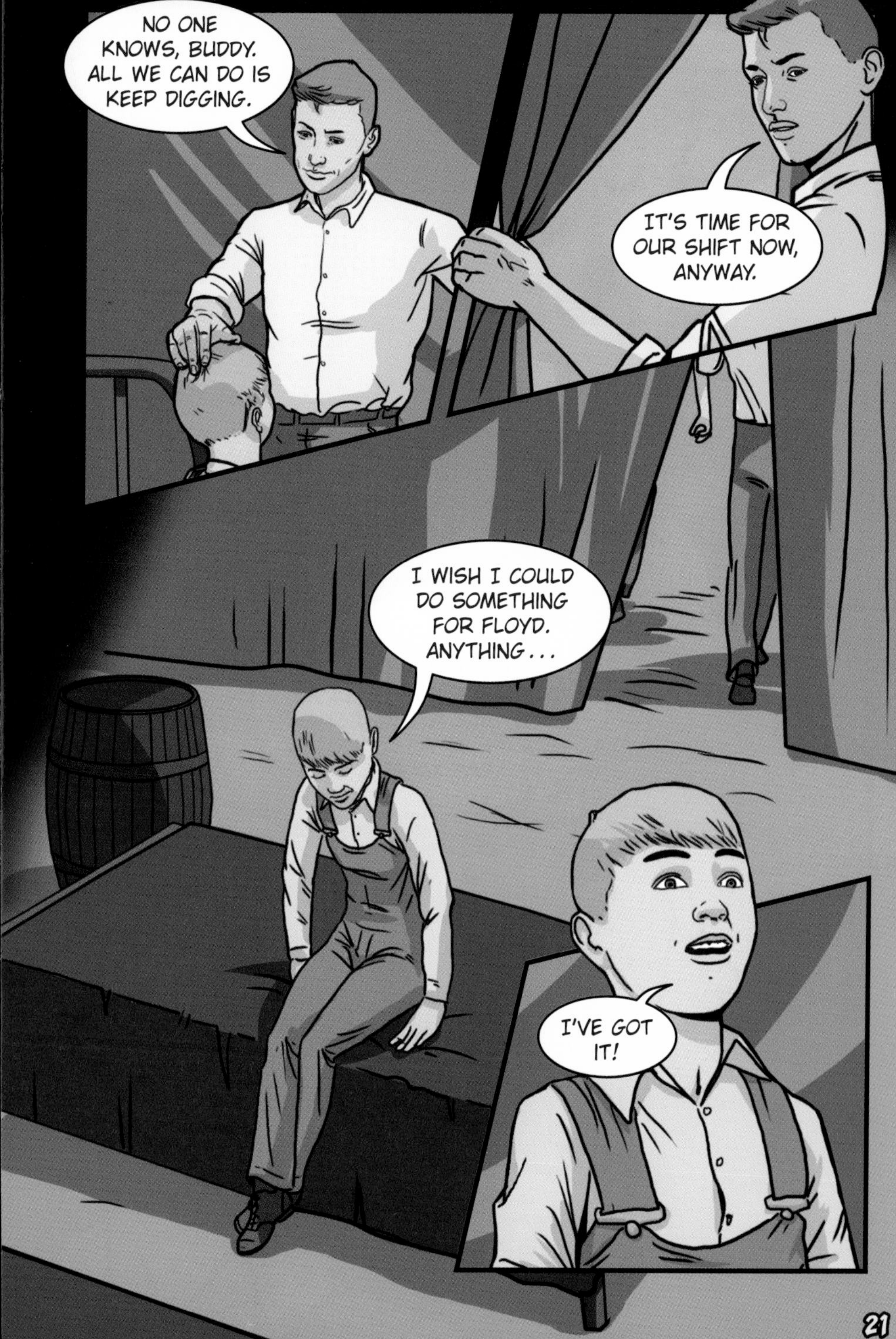
NO ONE KNOWS, BUDDY. ALL WE CAN DO IS KEEP DIGGING.
IT'S TIME FOR OUR SHIFT NOW, ANYWAY.
I WISH I COULD DO SOMETHING FOR FLOYD. ANYTHING...
I'VE GOT IT!

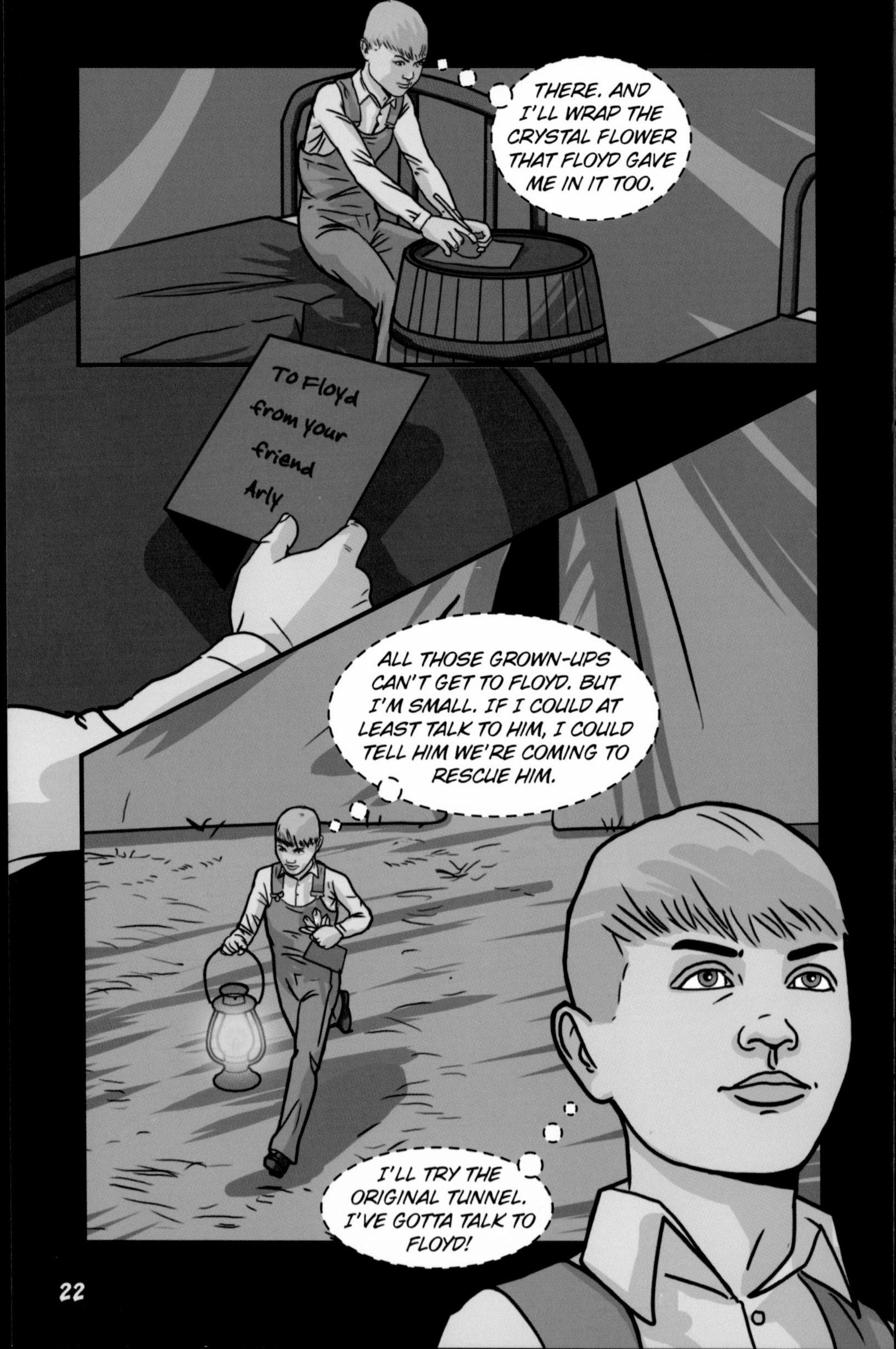
THERE. AND I'LL WRAP THE CRYSTAL FLOWER THAT FLOYD GAVE ME IN IT TOO.
To Floyd from your friend Arly
ALL THOSE GROWN-UPS CAN'T GET TO FLOYD. BUT I'M SMALL. IF I COULD AT LEAST TALK TO HIM, I COULD TELL HIM WE'RE COMING TO RESCUE HIM.
I'LL TRY THE ORIGINAL TUNNEL. I'VE GOTTA TALK TO FLOYD!

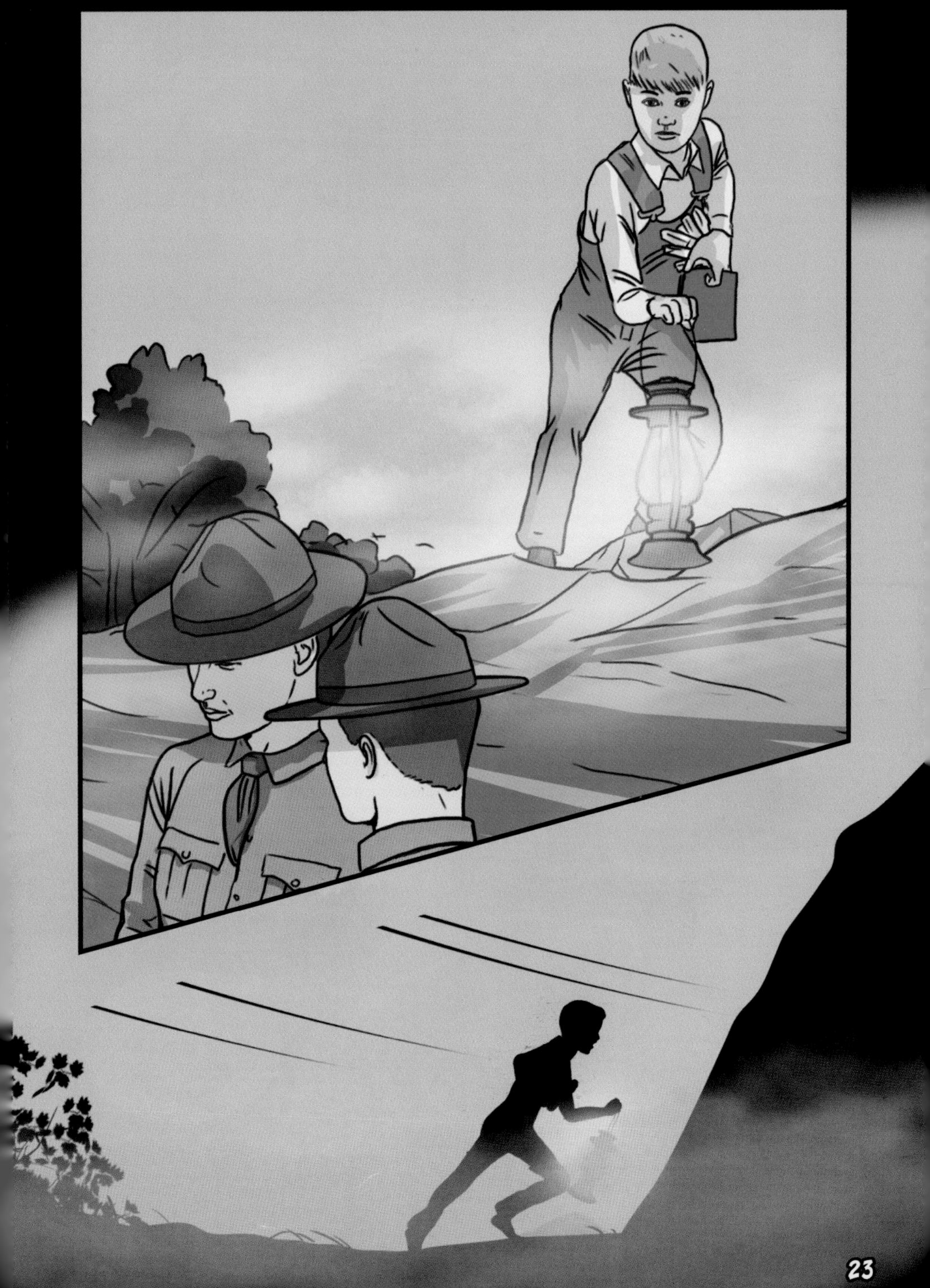

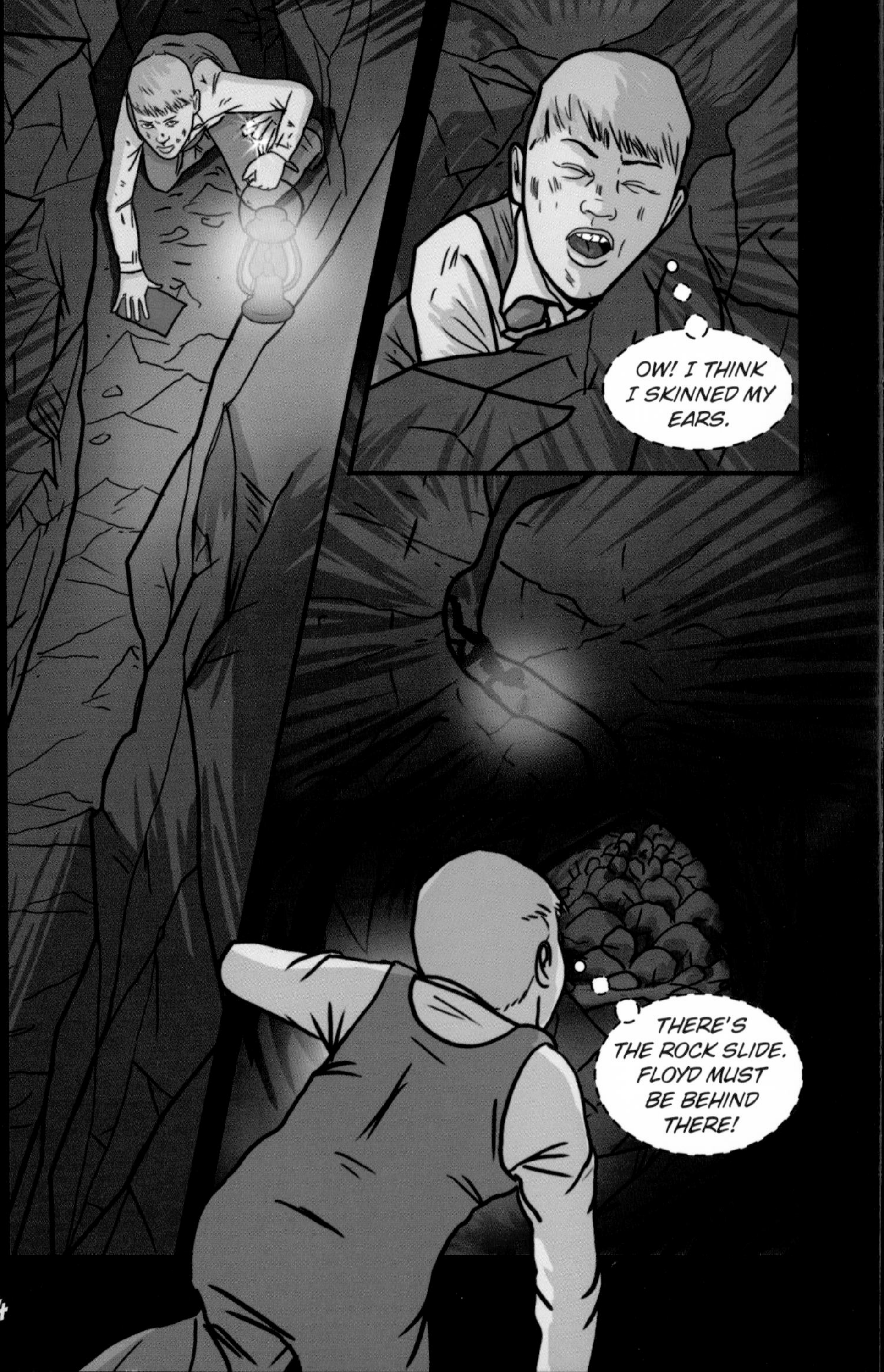
OW! I THINK I SKINNED MY EARS.
THERE'S THE ROCK SLIDE. FLOYD MUST BE BEHIND THERE!

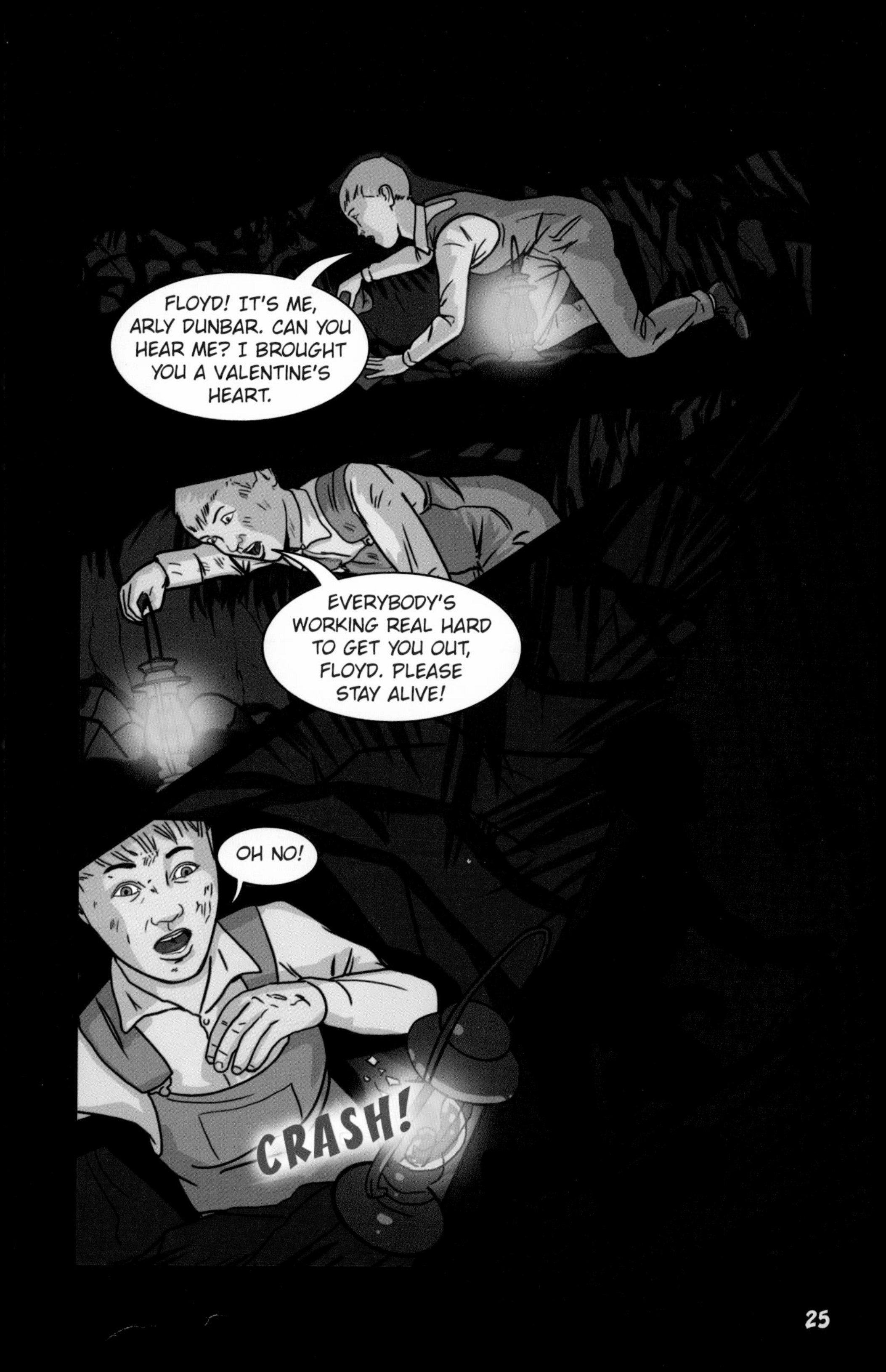
FLOYD! IT'S ME, ARLY DUNBAR. CAN YOU HEAR ME? I BROUGHT YOU A VALENTINE'S HEART.
EVERYBODY'S WORKING REAL HARD TO GET YOU OUT, FLOYD. PLEASE STAY ALIVE!
OH NO!
CRASH!

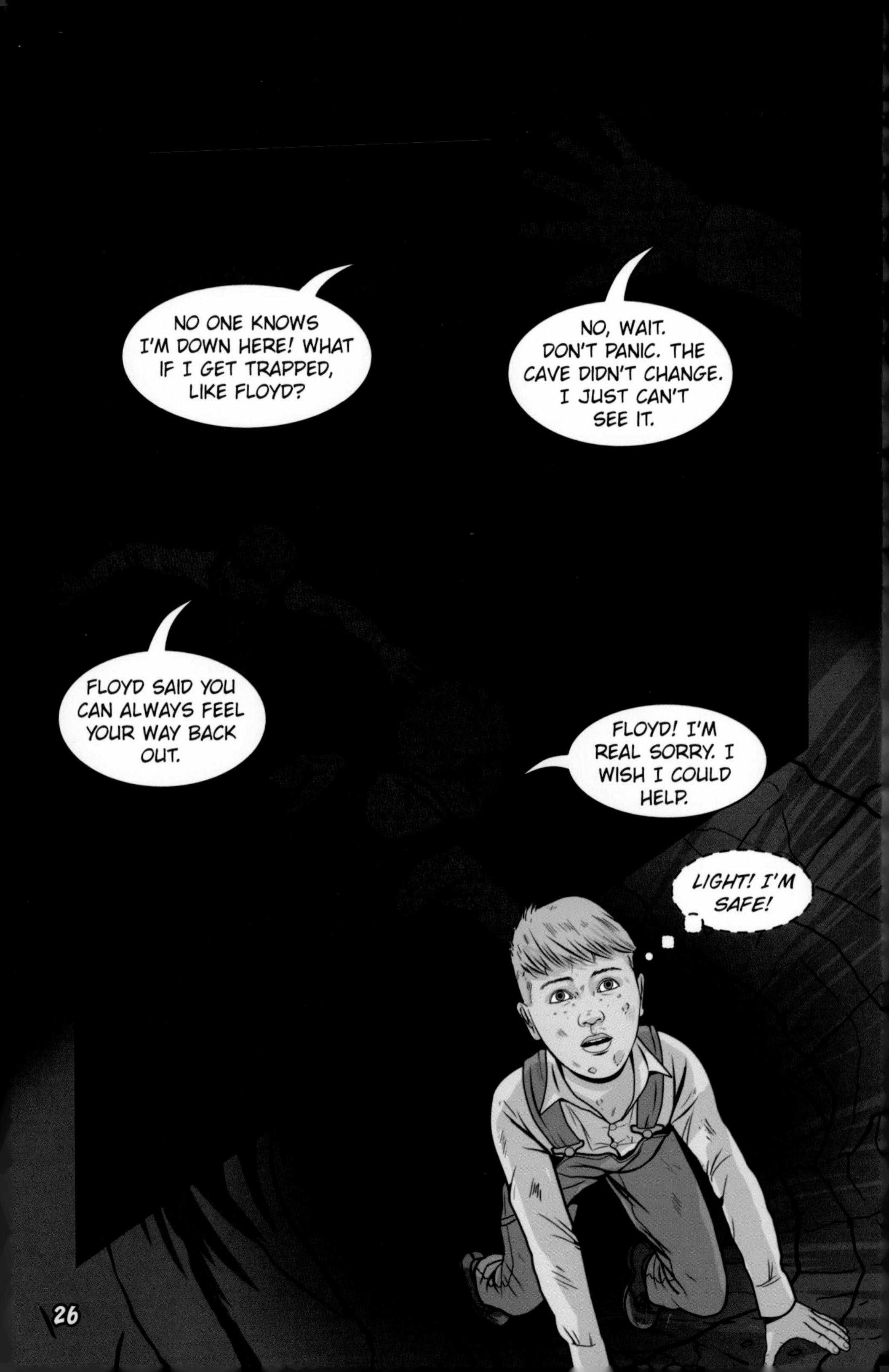
NO ONE KNOWS I'M DOWN HERE! WHAT IF I GET TRAPPED, LIKE FLOYD?
NO, WAIT. DON'T PANIC. THE CAVE DIDN'T CHANGE. I JUST CAN'T SEE IT.
FLOYD SAID YOU CAN ALWAYS FEEL YOUR WAY BACK OUT.
FLOYD! I'M REAL SORRY. I WISH I COULD HELP.
LIGHT! I'M SAFE!

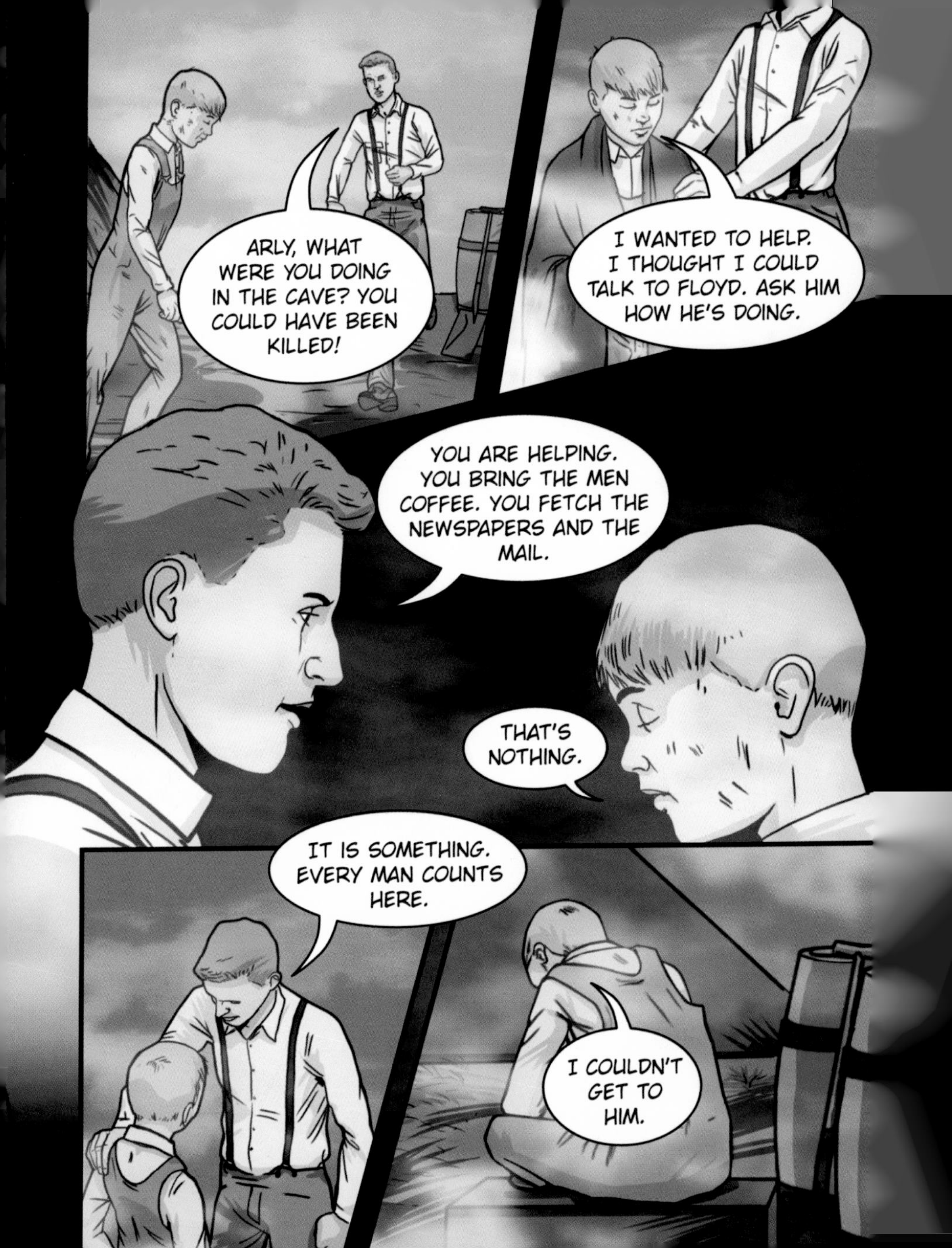
ARLY, WHAT WERE YOU DOING IN THE CAVE? YOU COULD HAVE BEEN KILLED!
I WANTED TO HELP. I THOUGHT I COULD TALK TO FLOYD. ASK HIM HOW HE'S DOING.
YOU ARE HELPING. YOU BRING THE MEN COFFEE. YOU FETCH THE NEWSPAPERS AND THE MAIL.
THAT'S NOTHING.
IT IS SOMETHING. EVERY MAN COUNTS HERE.
I COULDN'T GET TO HIM.

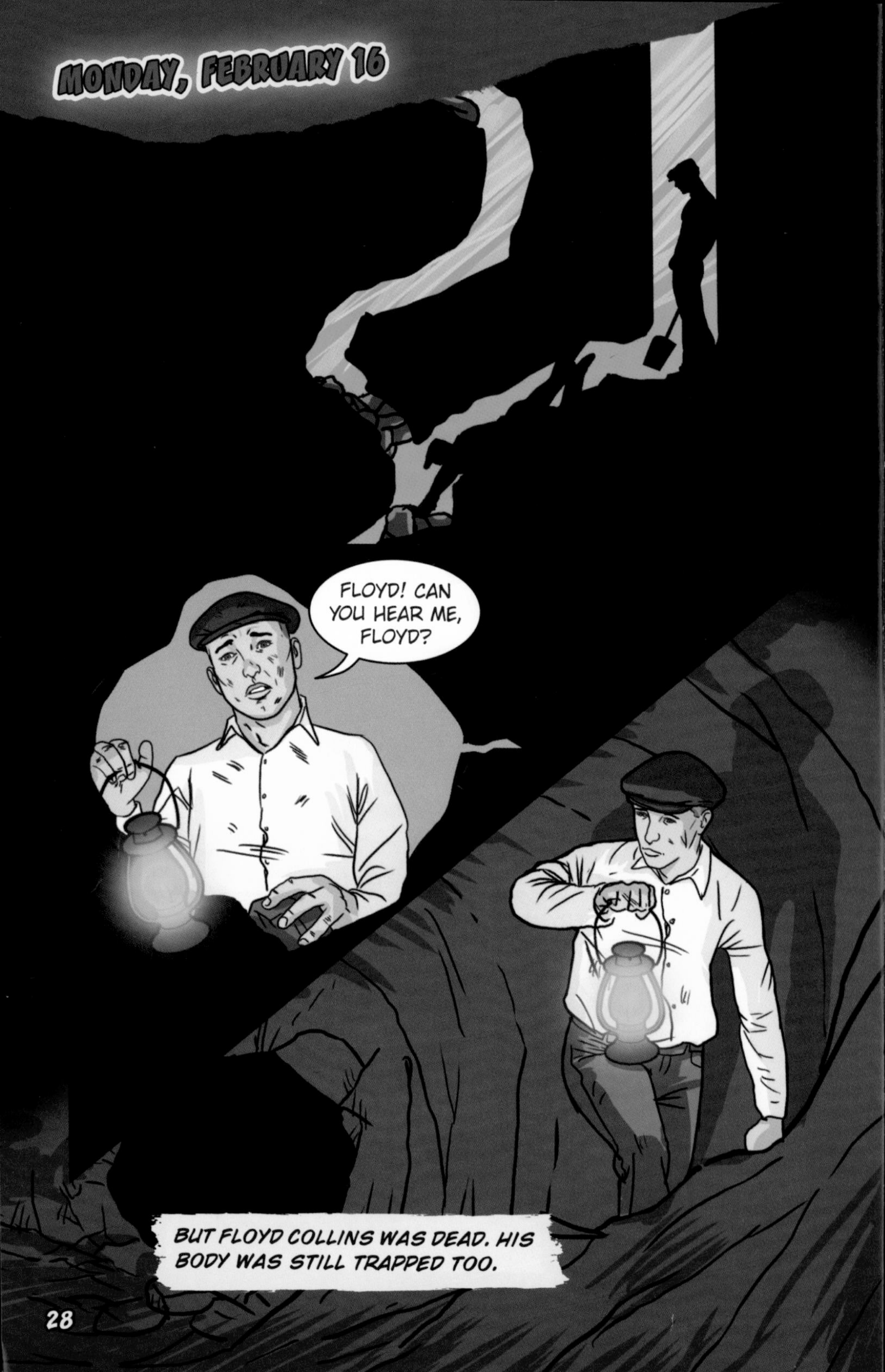
MONDAY, FEBRUARY 16
FLOYD! CAN YOU HEAR ME, FLOYD?
BUT FLOYD COLLINS WAS DEAD. HIS BODY WAS STILL TRAPPED TOO.

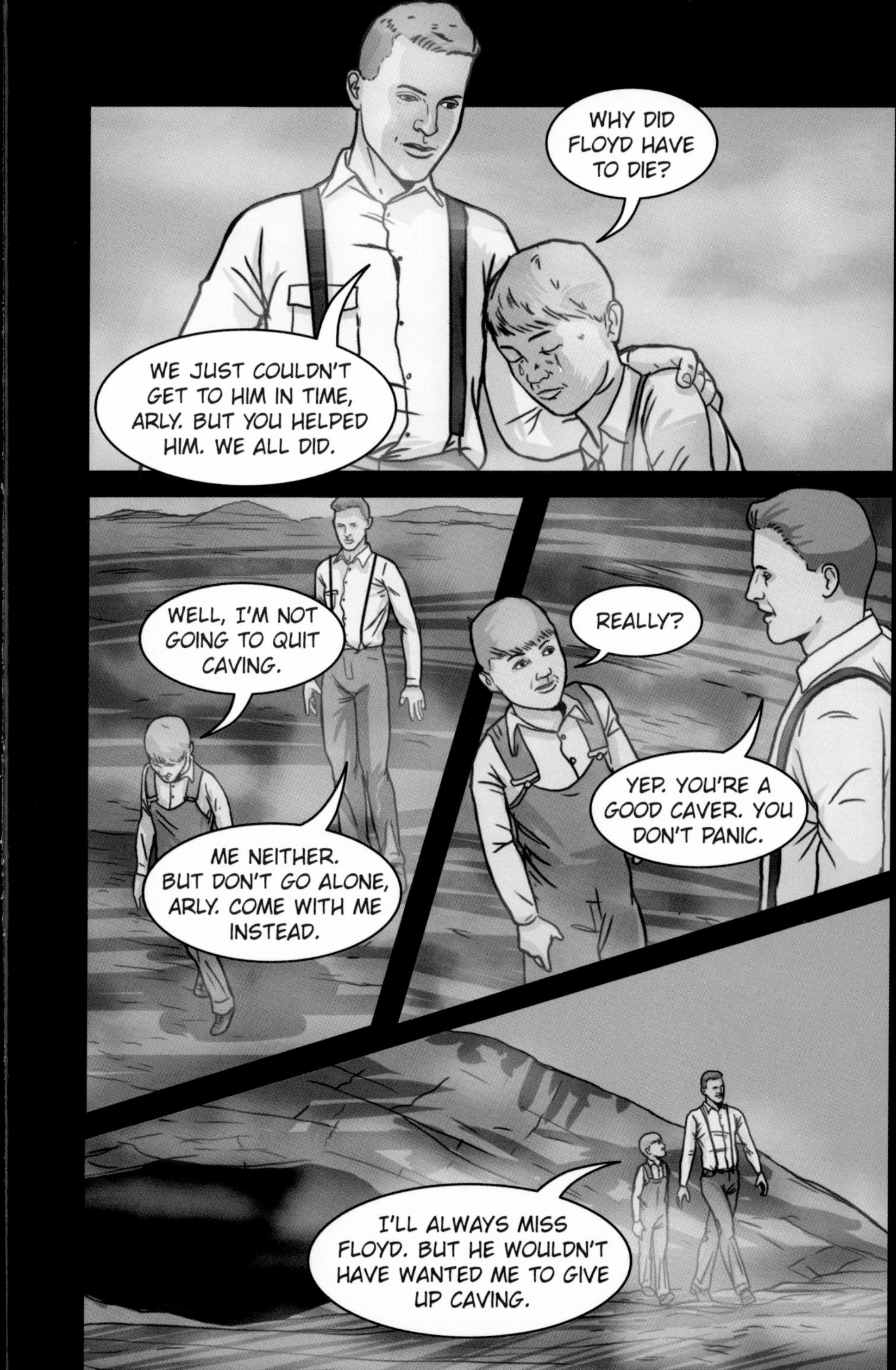
WHY DID FLOYD HAVE TO DIE?
WE JUST COULDN'T GET TO HIM IN TIME, ARLY. BUT YOU HELPED HIM. WE ALL DID.
WELL, I'M NOT GOING TO QUIT CAVING.
ME NEITHER. BUT DON'T GO ALONE, ARLY. COME WITH ME INSTEAD.
REALLY?
YEP. YOU'RE A GOOD CAVER. YOU DON'T PANIC.
I'LL ALWAYS MISS FLOYD. BUT HE WOULDN'T HAVE WANTED ME TO GIVE UP CAVING.

AFTERWORD

FLOYD'S FAMILY, FRIENDS, AND NEIGHBORS HONORED HIS MEMORY WITH A MEMORIAL SERVICE THE NEXT DAY. HIS BODY WAS RECOVERED IN THE SPRING. EVERYBODY REMEMBERED FLOYD COLLINS. HIS STORY APPEARED IN NEWSPAPERS ACROSS THE COUNTRY. REPORTERS TALKED ABOUT HIM ON THE RADIO. MUSICIANS EVEN WROTE SONGS ABOUT HIM.

FLOYD'S GRAVESTONE READS "GREATEST CAVE EXPLORER EVER KNOWN." TO THIS DAY, FLOYD'S COMMUNITY STILL CELEBRATES HIS MEMORY. EVERY YEAR, THE COMMUNITY HOLDS THE FLOYD COLLINS FESTIVAL. THERE ARE PLAYS AND FILMS ABOUT FLOYD. PEOPLE COME TO HEAR ABOUT HIS LIFE, LEARN ABOUT EXPLORING CAVES, AND DISCOVER DAILY LIFE IN THE 1920S.

TODAY, THE AREA AROUND SAND CAVE IS PART OF MAMMOTH CAVE NATIONAL PARK. WALKWAYS AND PERMANENT LIGHTS MAKE THE CAVES SAFE FOR PEOPLE TO VISIT. AND LIKE FLOYD, PEOPLE STILL FEEL AWE AND WONDER WHEN THEY ENTER KENTUCKY'S CAVES.

FURTHER READING AND WEBSITES

AMERICAN CAVE CONSERVATION ASSOCIATION: KID'S CAVE
HTTP://WWW.CAVERN.ORG/ACCA/KIDSCAVE.PHP

BROWN, DOTTIE. *KENTUCKY*. MINNEAPOLIS: LERNER PUBLICATIONS
COMPANY, 2002.

COOPER, SHARON KATZ. *CAVES AND CREVICES*. CHICAGO: RAINTREE,
2010.

HAYS, ANNA JANE. *THE SECRET OF THE CIRCLE-K CAVE*. NEW YORK: KANE
PRESS, 2006.

KENTUCKY SECRETARY OF STATE: ALL ABOUT KENTUCKY
HTTP://WWW.SOS.KY.GOV/KIDS/ALL/DEFAULT.HTM

KIDS WORLD SPORTS: SPELUNKING
HTTP://PBSKIDS.ORG/KWS/SPORTS/SPELUNKING.HTML

KRAMER, STEPHEN. *CAVES*. MINNEAPOLIS: FIRST AVENUE EDITIONS, 1995.

LINDOP, LAURIE. *CAVE SLEUTHS: SOLVING SCIENCE UNDERGROUND*.
MINNEAPOLIS: TWENTY-FIRST CENTURY BOOKS, 2006.

LYNETTE, RACHEL. *WHO LIVES IN A DEEP DARK CAVE?* NEW YORK:
POWERKIDS PRESS, 2011.

TAYLOR, PETER LANE, AND CHRISTOS NICOLA. *THE SECRET OF PRIEST'S
GROTTO: A HOLOCAUST SURVIVAL STORY*. MINNEAPOLIS: KAR-BEN
PUBLISHING, 2007.

WALKER, SALLY M. *CAVES*. MINNEAPOLIS: LERNER PUBLICATIONS
COMPANY, 2008.

ABOUT THE AUTHOR

CANDICE RANSOM HAS WRITTEN MANY AWARD-WINNING FICTION AND NONFICTION BOOKS FOR CHILDREN AND YOUNG ADULTS. SHE HOLDS A MASTER OF FINE ARTS IN WRITING FROM VERMONT COLLEGE. SHE LIVES IN FREDERICKSBURG, VIRGINIA.

ABOUT THE ADAPTER

EMMA CARLSON BERNE HAS WRITTEN AND EDITED MORE THAN TWO DOZEN BOOKS FOR YOUNG PEOPLE, INCLUDING BIOGRAPHIES OF SUCH DIVERSE FIGURES AS CHRISTOPHER COLUMBUS, WILLIAM SHAKESPEARE, THE HILTON SISTERS, AND SNOOP DOGG. SHE HOLDS A MASTER'S DEGREE IN COMPOSITION AND RHETORIC FROM MIAMI UNIVERSITY. MS. BERNE LIVES IN CINCINNATI, OHIO, WITH HER HUSBAND AND SON.

ABOUT THE ILLUSTRATORS

TED HAMMOND IS A CANADIAN ARTIST, LIVING AND WORKING JUST OUTSIDE OF TORONTO. HAMMOND HAS CREATED ARTWORK FOR EVERYTHING FROM FANTASY AND COMIC-BOOK ART TO CHILDREN'S MAGAZINES, POSTERS, AND BOOK ILLUSTRATION.

RICHARD PIMENTEL CARBAJAL HAS A BROAD SPECTRUM OF ILLUSTRATIVE SPECIALTIES. HIS BACKGROUND HAS FOCUSED ON LARGE-SCALE INSTALLATIONS AND SCENERY. CARBAJAL RECENTLY HAS EXPANDED INTO THE BOOK PUBLISHING AND ADVERTISING MARKETS.

Text copyright © 2012 by Candice F. Ransom
Illustrations © 2012 by Lerner Publishing Group, Inc.

Graphic Universe™ is a trademark of Lerner Publishing Group, Inc.

Graphic Universe™
A division of Lerner Publishing Group, Inc.
241 First Avenue North
Minneapolis, MN 55401 U.S.A.

Website address: www.lernerbooks.com

Berne, Emma Carlson.
    The underground adventure of Arly Dunbar, cave explorer / by Candice Ransom ; adapted by Emma Carlson Berne ; illustrated by Ted Hammond and Richard Pimentel Carbajal.
        p.   cm. — (History's kid heroes)
    Summary: When his friend, Floyd Collins, becomes trapped in a cave in Kentucky in 1925, ten-year-old Arly places himself in great danger while trying to help with the rescue operation.
    Includes bibliographical references.
    ISBN: 978–0–7613–6182–4 (lib. bdg. : alk. paper)
    1. Graphic novels. [1. Graphic novels. 2. Rescue work—Fiction. 3. Caves—Fiction. 4. Collins, Floyd, 1890–1925—Fiction. 5. Heroes—Fiction. 6. Sand Cave (Ky.)—Fiction. 7. Kentucky—History—20th century—Fiction. 8. Ransom, Candice F., 1952– Danger at Sand Cave—Adaptations.] I. Hammond, Ted, ill. II. Carbajal, Richard Pimentel, ill. III. Ransom, Candice F., 1952– Danger at Sand Cave. IV. Title.
    PZ7.7.B46Und 2012
    796.52'509769752—dc22   2010040722

Manufactured in the United States of America
1—BC—7/15/11